ALSO BY

ANNA GAVALDA

French Leave

Billie

LIFE,
ONLY BETTER

Anna Gavalda

LIFE,
ONLY BETTER

1. Mathilde
2. Yann

Translated from the French
by Tina Kover

Europa
editions

Europa Editions
214 West 29th Street
New York, N.Y. 10001
www.europaeditions.com
info@europaeditions.com

Library of Congress Cataloging in Publication Data is available
ISBN 978-1-60945-294-0

Gavalda, Anna
Life, Only Better

Book design by Emanuele Ragnisco
www.mekkanografici.com

Cover photo © WizData/iStock

Prepress by Grafica Punto Print – Rome

Printed in the USA

For Marianne

CONTENTS

LIFE,
ONLY BETTER

MATHILDE

ACT ONE

1.

A café near the Arc de Triomphe. I almost always sit in the same spot. In the back, to the left, behind the bar. I don't read. I don't move. I don't mess with my cell phone. I'm waiting for someone.

I'm waiting for someone who isn't coming, and I'm bored, so I watch the sun set over the Escale de l'Étoile.

Last co-workers, last drinks, last stale jokes; slack water for almost an hour, and then Paris finally stretches its legs. Taxis idle; girls come out of the woodwork. The boss dims the lights, and the waiters get younger. They put a little candle on each table—fake ones, that flicker but don't drip—and pressure me discreetly: have another drink, or beat it.

I have another drink.

This is the seventh time (not counting the first two) I've come to this dive to drink among the dogs and the wolves. I know because I've kept every single one of my bar tabs. At first I must have thought they'd make a nice souvenir; then I guess it was just habit, or some kind of fetishism, but now?

Now I know it's so I'll have something to grab onto when I put my hand in my coat pocket. I mean, if these pieces of paper exist, it proves that . . .

That what?

That nothing.

That life is dear, here by the Unknown Soldier.

2.

One o'clock in the morning. Still no luck. I'm going home.

I live near the Montmartre cemetery. I've never walked so much in my life. I had a bike—named Jeannot—but I lost it the other day. I'm not sure when, exactly. After a party at the house of some people I didn't know. They lived over by the Gare Saint-Lazare, I think.

Some guy had taken me back to his place. I was fine until we were in bed, and then I wasn't. The cat's litter box, the patterns on his quilt, the *Fight Club* poster above the Ikea bed . . . I . . . I just couldn't.

I held my liquor better than expected.

It was the first time that had happened to me; sobering up in one fell swoop like that, and it upset me. I'd have liked it, anyway—to just let go a little bit. I liked that. You could do worse than Brad Pitt and Edward Norton, as third wheels go. But my body let me down.

How was it possible?

My body.

My pretty body.

I wouldn't have admitted it then, but tonight, after all these miles of solitary walking, and this emptiness, and this nothing, and this lack of anything, of everything, everywhere, all the time, I can admit it. It was him.

He was the parasite, and I saw his energy-sucking for what it was, for the first time, between those ugly sheets.

Nude and disappointed, my back to the wall, I was puzzling over it when I heard a voice thickly reassuring me:

"Hey, you can stay anyway, okay?"

If I'd had a gun in my hand I'd have blown his head off for that *anyway*, for the contempt, the favor he was doing the bitch who hadn't sucked him off.

Bang.

I quivered with it. On the stairs, and out in the street, and while I looked for my bike under the streetlights. Quivered with rage. I'd never felt like that before.

My mouth tasted like puke, and I spat on the ground to get rid of it.

But I can't work up a gob of spit worthy of the name, and so I ended up drooling on myself, on my sleeve and my pretty scarf, and that was fine, because how else could I explain so much hate?

I was only living the way I deserved to, and I was living . . . *anyway*.

3.

My name is Mathilde Salmon. I'm twenty-four. Officially, I'm still a student in art history (the beautiful lie), but in real life I work for my brother-in-law. The rich, handsome, cool one. The one who's always rubbing his nose and never wears a tie. He runs a big digital design agency for web branding and development (translation: if you've got some shit to sell and you want to peddle it on the 'net, he'll whip you up a pretty storefront with signposting straight to the (secure) checkout), and he enticed me into working for him last year.

He needed someone to work for him and I needed spending money. It was my birthday and we shook hands over a drink. Could have been worse, as contracts go.

As a student, I get all kinds of price reductions at the movies and in museums, gyms, and restaurants that cater to the universities—but since I spend most of my time in front of a computer screen now, my IQ has gone way down. I'm making too much money to go back to student dining halls. I don't take advantage of any of that stuff very much anymore.

I work at home, at my own pace, and off the books. I've got a thousand names, a thousand addresses, a thousand pseudonyms, and at least that many avatars, and I write comments as phony as the day is long.

Think of the ticket inspector at the Lilas Metro station. Always the exact same spiel, right? I write the same stuff so often that I know it by heart.

J'fais des com', des p'tits com', encore des p'tits com',
Des com' d'seconde cla-a-ss-eu,
Des com' d'première cla-a-asse . . .

I get sent endless lists of sites followed by the notes "ruin them" or "praise only" (if it's cool it's always in English, in the digital world). It's basically all about tearing down potential clients and then building them back up again, before splashing positive reviews all over the discussion forums and giving them the best possible Google references—after they've forked over enough cash, of course.

I'll give you an example. The company Superyoyo.com manufactures and sells super yo-yos, but their website is total crap (for proof of this, see all the snarky comments left, dropped, shared, Yelped, tweeted, poked, tagged, requested, pinned, unliked, un-loled, or chatted everywhere you can think of by Micheline T. (me), Jeannotdu41 (myself), Choubi_angel (I), Helmutvonmunchen (Ich), or NYUbohemiangirls (yours truly and moi, dude), and voilà, total panic in Yoyoland. But as it turns out, Mr. and Mrs. Yoyo, who have been informed of my brother-in-law's wizardry thanks to a strategy as twisted as it is brilliant (too long and boring a story to tell here), fall for it and come begging: they absolutely *have* to have a brand-new shiny website! It's a matter of life or death for the business! So my brother-in-law, the great master, graciously agrees to help them, and three weeks later, a miracle! All you have to do is type "yo" or "yoy" in a search engine and bam, Yoyoland pops right up (it doesn't if you only type "y"; not yet, anyway, but we're working on that day and night). And then, another miracle! Micheline T. orders ten of everything for each of her six grandchildren; Jeannotdu41 is thrilled and is going to sing the praises of Superyoyo in all the yo-yo hot spots in the world; Choubi_angel says they're the coolest thing ever; Helmutvonmunchen vants to be a retailer uff dese yo-yos SCHNELL, and NYUbohemiangirls are sooooo excited cuz yo-yos are, like, sooooo French!

*

And that's it. That's all I do. I leave comments. And my brother-in-law, from his huge apartment in the 16th Arrondissement, looks to diversify again.

It's a fake good plan, not a real one, I know. I'd be better off finishing (starting) my master's thesis, "From Queen Wilhelmina of the Netherlands to Paul Jouanny: the history and design of watercolorists' trailers and other vehicles used by open-air painters" (quite a mouthful, eh?) or thinking about my future, my biological clock, and my retirement plan, but tough shit. I lost my faith somewhere along the way, and maybe I just want to live in the open air, too.

Because, I mean, everything's rigged. Everything's just comments. The ice caps are melting, and the rich are only getting richer while the small farmers are hanging themselves in their barns, and they're taking away the public benches to keep the bums from sitting on them. Frankly, I don't see why I should break my back to get ahead when the world's this fucked up.

So to forget it all, I play along with my brother-in-law and Larry Page: I lie from dawn 'til dusk, and I dance from dusk 'til dawn.

Well, I *used* to dance. These days I tighten my belt and hang around in the moonlight waiting for a guy who doesn't even know I'm waiting for him.

It's total bullshit.

I must really be ~~lost~~ ~~insecure~~ softhearted, to have gotten to this point.

4.

auline and Julie D., the two girls with whom I share a 110 m² apartment on Rue Damrémont, are twins. One of them works at a bank and the other one works for an insurance company. Rock 'n' roll attitude, man. We have zero in common, which is the secret of our successful cohabitation: I'm at home when they're not, and by the time they get home I'm gone.

They keep track of the bills and I sign for their packages (some PayPal bullshit). I bring home croissants and they take out the trash.

It's awesome.

Yeah, they're a bit airheaded, but I'm really glad they picked me to play the part of their roommate. They'd organized a series of auditions, like *In Search of the Next Practically-Perfect Roommate* (my God) (what an extravaganza) (yet another unforgettable episode in my crazy misspent youth) and I was the Chosen One, though I've never really understood why. At the time I was a ticket agent—and not only that, a guard, too! A security guard! At the Marmottan Museum. And I think the influence of good old Monet worked in my favor, because surely a neat and tidy young woman who spent so much time among the *Water Lilies* must be respectable.

Like I said, a bit airheaded.

This little stint in Paris is just something for them to put on their résumés. They don't really like it here and can't wait to move back to Roubaix, where Mommy and Daddy and their cat Tickles still live, and where they run off to as often as possible. So I'll take advantage of my good luck (a great apartment all to myself every weekend, and the stock of neatly-folded microfiber baby wipes they keep under the sink, so handy for cleaning up my friends' vomit) until they decide to move back to the country for good.

Well, let's say I *used to* take advantage of it. Now . . . I'm not so sure. They're really starting to get on my nerves—they wear Isotoner ballerina slippers around the house and listen to Chante France at breakfast; it's hard sometimes—but I'm well aware the real problem is me. They're always quiet, making sure to turn the volume down when I start to get lost in the steam from their instant coffee. I've got nothing to reproach them with.

No; I and no one else am to blame for my own trouble. It's been almost three months now since I enjoyed anything, or went out, or had a drink.

Since I went wrong.

* * *

Three months ago, the apartment was still a construction site.

It was in a bad state of repair, and Pauline (the less scatter-brained twin) had convinced our landlord to let us renovate the place in exchange for a suspension of the rent equivalent to the final cost of the project (a complicated way of putting it that I didn't come up with, I can assure you). Pauline and Julie were as excited as little kids about the whole thing, making lists of prices, drawing up plans, leafing through catalogues, and requesting loads of quotes, which they spent whole evenings discussing while sipping herbal tea. I wondered if maybe they'd both chosen the wrong profession.

All the commotion had irritated me, and I'd been forced to

leave the apartment in search of peace and quiet, churning out comments in my brother-in-law's beehive instead, alongside all the Geeks, Version 2.0—not ideal, but better than our place, where the electricity left a lot to be desired (my computer screen flickered if we turned on the stove), the paint was flaking, and the bathroom wasn't exactly convenient (we constantly had to step over an old bidet). I didn't take responsibility for anything, and when the girls suggested to me that we pay for the renovations in cash to get back the VAT (at least!) and ingratiate ourselves with Mr. Carvalho (businessman, Freemason, sly old fox, and in way over his head), I didn't need to be asked twice.

I'm not timid when it comes to those things, either.

Why am I telling you all this? Because without the subtle blackmail of that man, so "overrrrwhelmed" by his social benefits charges; without the sudden VAT increase on the building, and without our greed—all of us, but him most of all—I wouldn't be here, in this depressing neighborhood, waiting and watching for my nonexistent someone.

This is what happened.

5.

A café near the Arc de Triomphe. I was sitting in the back, to the left, behind the bar. I wasn't reading. I wasn't budging. I wasn't messing with my cell phone. I was waiting for Julie.

My roommate, the one who works at BNP (or BNP Paribas, as she's always careful to say), and who's calculating everything that can be divided up among us, down to the smallest decimal point (rent, utilities, bonuses, contracts, tips, detergent tabs, firefighters calendar, toilet paper, shower gel, welcome mat, and so on and so forth and even more ridiculous).

We'd agreed to meet late that Friday afternoon in a bar close to where she worked. It had annoyed me a bit to go all the way across Paris just to please her, but I knew she had a train to catch, and besides, I was the . . . uh, let's just say "least hardworking" . . . of the three of us.

She was supposed to give me their two-thirds of the money for our favorite tax-evading mason, whom I was meeting the next morning. A nice fat envelope stuffed with 10,000 euros in cash.

Well, anyway . . . it was Versailles.

I'd decided to take advantage of the afternoon playing hooky to hit the shops; back then I was still a petite brunette, as normal as you could possibly imagine—stupid, happy, shallow, and extravagant—and while I waited for Julie I went nuts over frilly handbags, accessories, beauty products, and countless pairs of impractical shoes perched all around me on the moleskin bench.

I'd shopped miles of windows, and now I was sipping a mojito to get myself under control.

I was exhausted and completely broke. Shamefaced and deliriously happy.

The girls would understand.

* * *

She arrived right on the dot in her little mouse-grey suit. She didn't have time for a drink; well, okay, fine, but just a mineral water. She waited for the server to leave, glanced around warily, and finally pulled an envelope out of her messenger bag, handing it to me with the mournful look bank tellers always get when they're forced to give you any money.

"Aren't you going to put it in your purse?" she asked worriedly.

"Oh—yeah, yeah, of course. Sorry."

"It's quite a bit of cash, that's all."

Watching me stir the mint leaves around in my drink didn't seem to make her feel much better. "You'll be careful with it, won't you?"

I nodded gravely (poor thing, if only she knew. It would take more than a little rum and lime juice to turn my head) and stuffed the money into my bag, which I kept in my lap to reassure her.

"It's all in hundreds. At first I put it in one of the bank's envelopes, but then I realized that wasn't very discreet. Because of the logo, you know. So I changed it."

"Good thinking," I said, nodding.

"But I didn't seal it, so you could put in your share."

"Perfect." She still wasn't relaxing. "It'll be fine, Julie," I sighed, slipping the strap of my purse over my head. "Look, just like a Saint Bernard, see? The charming Antonio will get his money, I promise. Don't worry."

Her mouth twitched a little, in a smile or maybe a sigh; hard to tell. She reached for the check.

"Leave it; it's on me," I said. "You'd better go, or you'll miss your train. Give your parents a hug for me and tell Pauline her package came."

She stood up, threw one last anxious look at my beat-up carrier bag, belted herself into her trench coat, and left almost regretfully for her weekend at home.

Only then, in that café near the Arc de Triomphe, sitting in the back, et cetera, did I reach for my phone. Marion had left me a message asking if I'd splurged on the little blue dress we'd spotted together the week before, and if I was still over-drawn on my bank account, and if I had any plans tonight.

I called her back and we giggled like crazy. I told her about my haul—*no little blue dress, but a to-die-for pair of heels, some adorable barrettes, and the most gorgeous undies—yeah, a bra like the ones from Eres, with cups like this and straps like that, and these fantastic little panties—I swear!—not expensive at all and just too cute, yep, you know, the kind that say you're really a minx under those conservative clothes*, blah blah blah, hee hee hee, ooh la la.

Next I told her about my anal-retentive roommate and the saga of the envelope without a logo and how I hung my Upla around my neck like a goddamn overgrown Girl Scout to make Julie feel better, which of course made us laugh even harder.

Finally we talked about serious things: the plan for that evening, and who would be there, and what we should wear. And, of course, we had to discuss every single eligible guy we knew in great detail, down to the mileage on their cars, the wear on their tires, their family situations and marketable skills, and whether they were worth considering as boyfriends or not.

All that chatter made me thirsty, and I'd ordered another mojito to keep up my strength.

"What are you crunching on?" demanded my friend. Crushed ice, I told her. "Ugh, how can you do that?" she'd asked, horrified, and I made some stupid double-entendre about the benefits of liking to chew ice in certain situations.

It was all just bluster, of course. Pure, pathetic bravado; just something stupid I said to make my friend laugh, something I forgot as soon as it was out of my mouth. But it would come back to haunt me a few days later, and plunge me into complete terror.

You'll understand why soon enough.

Marion had hung up, and I'd dropped some cash on the table and grabbed my bags. It wasn't until I was out on the street, rummaging for my keys to unlock my bike, that I started to lose it.

I had everything else—the shoes, the antiwrinkle cream, the polka-dot panties—but I was missing the only bag that really counted.

"Shit," I murmured, "I'm such a fucking idiot," and I started retracing my steps as fast as I could, hurling abuse at myself the whole time.

6.

I was dripping with sweat all of a sudden. Cold sweat, little drops of it trickling down my spine. My legs had gone all wobbly too, and it was like I could hardly walk, as if the ground were crumbling away under my feet.

But I kept trying to talk myself down.

I muttered to myself as I ran frantically back across the street, ignoring the crosswalk and the blaring horns of irritated drivers: *Come on now, it's only been a few minutes, I'm just a block away. It's still there. The waiter will have noticed it when he came back to get his (generous) tip, he's put it aside for me and he'll hand it back to me in two minutes, rolling his eyes, like,* women! . . .

Calm down. Calm down.

I barely avoided getting mown down in the street, and I didn't calm down at all.

The bench seat was still warm, the impression of my thighs still visible. My money still lying on the table. My bag, gone.

7.

The servers were clueless. The manager was clueless. No, they hadn't seen anything, but hey, it wasn't surprising in this part of town. Someone had stolen their soap dishes only last week. Yes, that's right—soap dishes. Unbelievable, right? They'd been unscrewed from the wall. What a world we're living in. Not to mention the potted plants on the terrace, which they had to chain down every night. And the silverware! You wouldn't believe how much of that goes missing every year! Go on, see if you can guess.

Of course, I didn't hear a word of their babbling complaints. I didn't give a shit. I was in a state of total panic, and if they hadn't seen anyone leave after I did, it meant that the thief was still around the bar somewhere.

I combed the room and the terrace, scrutinizing the benches, the seats, customers' laps; looking under tables and on coatracks. I bumped into people, apologized, choked back tears. Searched the bathrooms, men's and women's; opened doors marked "Staff Only." Barged into the kitchens, asked questions, pushed back when anyone tried to give me shit. Begged, promised, melted down, swore, smiled, joked, explained, scanned, zoomed in, watched the front door, and finally resigned myself: there was no bag and no suspect to be found.

Someone was lying to me. Either that, or I'd lost my mind.

It was possible. Had already happened, probably. I couldn't think anymore; my head was spinning. Had I lost it on the way to my bike? Had the shoulder strap of my bag broken to punish me for making fun of the Girl Scouts? Had I been the victim of some expert pickpocket on the Champs-Élysées? Was this my afternoon away from the funny farm where I lived during the rest of the week?

I finally left the bar to the depressing accompaniment of their efforts to be helpful: "Really sorry, young lady. Leave us your phone number just in case. And check all the trash cans in the area. They only care about the money, you know; they always dump the rest right away. Wait a little while before you file a police report, though of course IDs are worth their weight in gold these days. With all the Gypsies hanging around on the Champs in the last couple of years, nothing should really be a surprise anymore . . .

"Anyway, best of luck."

As soon as I was outside I burst into tears.

At myself. At my stupidity. At the ridiculous shopping bags still looped over my arms. All this stuff I didn't need, didn't give a damn about, weighing me down . . .

And my lucky charms, and all my little bits and pieces, and my photos . . . and my phone, and my pretty makeup bag, and my keys, and my address—and my address along with my keys—and the locks would have to be changed, and the girls, who were far away and weren't very understanding about this kind of thing anyway—and my bank card, and my wallet that I loved so much, and my money, and *their* money. Christ, their money—ten thousand euros! Ten thousand euros, which I was supposed to give to that guy tomorrow morning! How goddamn worthless could I be? Oh, I was great at chattering on the phone with Marion, a total champion at that, but give me one important thing to do and this is what happens.

What had I done? What should I do? What was my name?

Why was I so overwhelmed? Why? And where would it end? Where was the Seine? Mom. Virgin Mary. God, help me.

Please, God. I promise I'll . . . Jesus, Mary, and Joseph, I know it doesn't seem like it but really I think about you all the time, and . . . Ten thousand fucking euros! What the hell is *wrong* with me? Why am I such an idiot? Saint Anthony—Saint Anthony of Padua . . . please reveal all your little hiding places . . . have pity on me. My photos, my phone, my archived messages, my contacts, my memories, my life, my friends . . . and now my bike. My chained-up bike, which looked at me like I was a moron and decided to get stolen too! And I don't even have the money to get a taxi, much less pay back the de Rochefort girls. My God—my bank card, and my PIN, and the emergency phone number to call to stop payment . . . and my friends, and my unlimited movie pass, and the video of Louison's first steps, and my Dior mascara, and my Coco rouge . . . and my day planner, the office keys, the Fotomat picture of me and Philou that I love so much, from the Hyper U store in Plancoët . . . and my little address book, which I loved, and all the memories in it, and my nail file . . . and the ten thousand euros . . . and . . .

And I cried.

A lot.

Too much.

Sometimes, a few tears just open the floodgates for all the others. I cried so much. I cried it all out. I cried for everything I didn't like about myself, for all the stupid things I'd done that I hadn't confessed, and for everything I'd lost since I was old enough to understand that some things went away forever.

I cried from the Place de l'Étoile to the Place de Clichy.

I cried all the way across Paris. I cried for my life.

8.

The concierge had a duplicate key. I could have kissed her. I even patted her dog in gratitude. I used our landline to cancel my bank card, riffled through the "Renovation" file for phone numbers, and left a message for Senhor Carvalho to buy a little time (I was overjoyed, in the midst of my misery, by my luck at getting his voicemail)—though I doubt he understood more than a word or two of my babbling. Didn't matter, since I was unreachable at the moment anyway. I double-locked the front door, sent a desperate e-mail to Marion, took a shower, rummaged through the twins' stuff, filched a couple of their sleeping pills, wrapped my nervous wreck of a self in the duvet, and closed my eyes, repeating Scarlett O'Hara's ridiculous words over and over in my head: *Tomorrow is another day.*

Sure it is, lady, sure it is.

Tomorrow's going to be a lot worse.

I wanted to die. It's stupid, I know; it's not like two sleeping pills can cause miraculous things to happen, but that's what I wanted that night: my mom at my bedside, singing me a lullaby and stroking my temples, forever and ever.

I hummed to myself instead—you know, to complete the nervous breakdown—and when I ran out of tears I went in search of a couple of bottles of wine to help me work up some more.

* * *

It had already taken everything I had in me to borrow three thousand euros from my brother-in-law, to complete my share of the money we owed. I couldn't imagine asking him for ten thousand more. I'd already had to listen to his little fables about squirrels and grasshoppers and ants. He hadn't said anything nasty; just a bit condescending, which was much worse. Almost fatherly.

I didn't like being talked to as if I were a child. My mom died when I was seventeen, and Arthur Rimbaud can go to hell with his *bocks* and his *limonade*; you can, in fact, become very serious at that age. The trick is not to show it. You keep on going, like an empty sack; you might buy all kinds of crap to compensate for the hollowness, but you will always lose what matters the most. It's sad, yeah, but it's just how it is, and you muddle through like everyone else. Sermons, on the other hand? Fuck that. I can't deal with that shit anymore. People who know everything and want to explain life to me? I cut them off at the root.

Sitting on the kitchen floor in the dark, my back against the oven door, I left it to Mr. Gordon and Madam Smirnoff to take the edge off my pain. I wasn't about to go off into some kind of psychotic delirium, but when *she* died I just had to grit my teeth and bear it (did I have a choice?), and the loss of my bag, which belonged to her, and was full of ties and tokens and memories and all kinds of little sweet irreplaceable things, finally allowed me to grieve for her.

I laughed, I blew my nose, I laughed some more. I mumbled things about my bag that didn't mean anything. It was like a cathar . . . a cath . . . caf . . . fafar . . . fsis . . . it . . . my . . . like a dam . . .

I let everything out.
Everything.
Everything.
Everything.

9.

I woke up at 1:38 in the afternoon, according to the oven clock, with quite a hangover. Maybe the most impressive one in my whole collection.

I was curled up in a ball on the kitchen floor. My eyes followed the cracks between the tiles, counting the dust bunnies under the furniture. *Hmm*, I thought, *there's that little knife we thought we'd thrown away with the orange peels . . .*

How long had I spent like that? Hours. Hours and hours. The sun was already slanting into the living room. Our pretty living room, all brand new, that we hadn't finished paying for.

Hang on a minute, Madam Chaos. Just let me spend a moment or two with my head in the wastebasket and then I'll go to the police station, I promise. I'll let my dear roommates know what's happened, and call my brother-in-law. I'll say *Hey, I've got a good one for you, bro! I need another 10,000! Now, now, be nice. I'll write idiotic comments for you for the next hundred and fifty years, to pay you back what I owe you.* That's all I'm good at, anyway. Being an anonymous nobody, and talking nonsense.

I was in the Marevskis' garden in La Varenne. My mother was explaining why we couldn't cut the tiny white cyclamens that grew at the foot of the lime trees.

"It's so new ones can grow, do you see?"

She'd already told me that hundreds of times, but I was so thrilled to see her again that I didn't dare interrupt her. And then we heard loud noises in the distance. *Is that thunder?* she asked, worried. *No*, I said, laughing. *It's the renovations, remember? They're knocking down everything in the apartment, so . . .*

Someone was hammering on the door. Shit, what time was it? Now the doorbell was ringing, and there were shouts, a horrible goddamn racket. Oh, my head. I stood up. I had a . . . something . . . stuck to my cheek. A bread crumb. 6:44 in the evening. Christ, I'd spent the whole day under the kitchen sink. *Ow*, fucking U-bend . . .

"Open up or I'm calling the fire department," screamed the voice.

The concierge. She was flipping out. This was the third time she'd come to the door. She'd been trying to call me since this morning. My roommates hadn't been able to reach me either, and kept bothering her in her office.

"And since I kept insisting to them that you were at home, they got worried, you see? They thought you'd had some kind of accident. My God, what a hassle! You've worried us all so much!"

My father had called them. My father, who I hadn't spoken to in years, but who was still in my phone's contact list as "Dad" out of pure weakness or some leftover shred of daughterly devotion, or something. Finally realizing that I was only half-awake and that her words were going in one ear and out the other, Mrs. Starovi reached out and took my arm, shaking it gently.

"Someone found your bag." Her eyes widened and she let me go. "Why are you crying? Come now, there's no reason to cry like that. Everything works out in this life, you see."

I was bawling too hard to agree with her. I tried to get hold of myself, to reassure her, but I could tell she thought I was crazy, and even as I gave her a snot-smeared smile I could hear a tiny voice in the depths of my jumbled-up mind saying, "Thank you. Oh, thank you, Mom."

10.

I called them back up there in the Great White North and by some fluke I got Pauline; otherwise I was still good for the trial of the asbestos Vase of Soissons. That being said, I got a pretty lukewarm reception, complete with heavy sighs, short snippy sentences, and tight-lipped little responses. It annoyed me so much that I ended up feeding her a huge lie (I know, I know, I'm worthless. It's my job.) instead of telling her to go fuck herself like I wanted to. I'd had enough emotions for the day. I just said in a tired voice that she didn't need to speak to me like I was a half-wit; that their envelope wasn't in my bag anymore, and that their cash was safe and sound. Everything's fine. End of story.

Hahahaha . . . that calmed her down immediately, the little dear. Her voice turned ten degrees warmer and her explanations got a lot clearer. Of course I listened to the very important stuff she had to tell me, but I knew at that exact moment that our careful years of *entente cordiale* were over, and I'd be leaving the Rue Damrémont as soon as possible. Life was too short, and I'd rather exile myself to the suburbs (gross) than keep living with people who got their kicks from frowning disapprovingly at me.

I don't give a shit about morals or moralizers. They can go fuck themselves. Especially when the holy fire that drives them, their homilies and sermons and their noble wrath, is measured in banknotes.

I know that's a fancy sentence full of bells and whistles

straight out of a Victor Hugo novel, but it rang hollow in my poor head, because those 10,000 euros had vanished into thin air and I'd stopped believing in Santa Claus a long time ago. The guy who called the number marked "Dad" in my phone's address book found my bag, yes, but he wouldn't be returning it to me fully loaded.

Nope.

Everything had worked out, yeah, but it was a big leap from there to saying that life was all rainbows and buttercups.

Where was I going to find that fucking money? Bang, I was back in the meat grinder again—except that it was okay, because this was something tangible, and I don't give a damn about tangible things.

Tangible things don't die in a hospital bed.

The only hitch was that the guy had told my dad—who had told my two airheaded roommates—that he wouldn't be in Paris over the long weekend (Monday was a bank holiday), and that I should meet him in the café where I'd left my bag, but not until next Tuesday at around 5:00 in the afternoon.

At first I was annoyed by his nerve—he could have just given it to the bar manager—but then I told myself it might be because of the cash that he hadn't wanted to risk it. The envelope was open, after all. And, pathetically, I started believing in Santa Claus again.

Then I went over to Marion's and we celebrated my resurrection.

In a dignified way, of course.

11.

The next three days were strange. The girls had scheduled their leave (yeah, they were twenty-eight years old and still spent their days off together, with their parents and Tickles) so I was alone until Tuesday evening.

I spun my wheels, waiting. For someone, something; some relief, or disappointment.

A story.

I threw myself into tasks I would never have cared about normally: straightening up, cleaning, mail, ironing. I sorted clothes, papers, books, CDs, listening to tracks and rereading pages along the way. I didn't turn on my laptop. I kept my hands busy to trick my mind. I pulled out my coursework and thesis notes, and rediscovered a series of sketches I'd made at the Compiègne transportation museum, on a beautiful autumn day about a hundred years ago. The softness of my highlighting strokes took me back.

I asked myself why I'd given it up. They were nice, my tales of trailers—and they saved me the shame of adding my idiotic efforts to all the ones art had already inspired. Why was I selling yo-yos instead? Why was I calling myself Choubi_angel and writing moronic comments punctuated by ridiculous emojis?

Why hadn't I gone yet to visit the stables of the Het Loo palace in Apeldoorn, to admire Queen Wilhelmina's pretty little watercolor paint box and her white funeral carriage? Why :-(:-/ :'-(?

I learned to live without calls or texts, without messages or voicemail. Without the security blanket of a "yes" or "no."

I learned to deal with the ennui of my day-to-day existence, and even to find a kind of pleasure in it. Before you knew it I'd be making jam and embroidering. I was distracted. I rambled around. I thought about . . . well, about this guy who'd gone away for the weekend with a little bit of me slung over his shoulder. I wondered how old he was; if he was introverted, well-educated, curious; if he'd tried other numbers before my father's; if he'd scrolled through my photos, his thumb stroking the screen of my phone. I wondered if he'd flipped through my address book, looked at the head shot on my ID card or the one on my driver's license, where I still had a shaved head (and was dressed entirely in funereal black, of course)—or the one on my student ID, where I looked like I was on my way to take communion at La Madeleine. I wondered if he'd found my Hello Kitty condoms, my under-eye concealer, my four-leaf clover, my secrets . . .

Was he dissecting the contents of my bag right then, even as I thought about him? And the ten thousand euros; had he counted it? Was he planning on helping himself to a commission for services rendered? Would he pretend to be surprised? *What's what? There was an envelope, you say? Don't ask me, I didn't touch anything.* I expected that, actually, because if he'd found my bag right after I left the bar, why hadn't he caught up with me in the street? I hadn't been walking very fast, after all; I'd had two mojitos in my belly and my whole life ahead of me . . .

Why?

Was he slow? Preoccupied? Some kind of weirdo? And where had he been sitting? Why hadn't I noticed him—after all, I loved nothing better than to people-watch while slowly getting tipsy . . .

A long, quiet, restless Easter weekend in an apartment I used to love but couldn't bear to live in anymore, hours spent in silence and reconciliation while waiting for a rendezvous I was both obsessed with and indifferent to.

It was the first time in years that I'd dreamed of my mom, seen her with her hair down and heard her voice. That gift was worth ten thousand euros and just as many tears, and if I'd known, I would have lost her bag a long time ago . . .

12.

Of course, looking back I can see that the trouble started on Tuesday at around . . . one o'clock, I'd say. I could ask myself, innocent flower that I am, why I spent so much time making myself pretty, creaming and gelling and spraying and powdering. Why I put on a dress, and then changed into trousers, and then back into a dress again, and why I made sure to have smooth skin and bare arms and red lips that day.

Yes, Mathilde, why?

Tyranny. The tyranny of the embittered. I was pretty because I was cheerful, and I was cheerful because I was happy. It didn't actually matter that much that my guardian angel was a man (as far as I knew) (a *guy*, Pauline had repeated; "a *guy* found your bag in the bar where you'd been"); you could have told me an old lady had found it, or the runtiest little weakling, and I'd have gotten ready with the same care. It wasn't him I was honoring by going into the city in a short little skirt; it was life. Life and its rare goodness, and the spring, and reunions. I was pretty because I was grateful.

Mathilde . . .
Okay—fine, yes, I was *also* pretty because it was a date. Made over the telephone, yes, and self-serving, yes, but serendipitous.

It was a date that had fallen out of the sky, with a human

being who was immediately desirable—a date in Paris, near the huge fairy-tale hall built by Emperor Napoleon I, at teatime, for reasons of integrity.

I was pretty because it was a hell of a lot more exciting than some online date; I mean, shit!

There, now you know everything, Doctor.

I stopped to buy flowers near the Parc Monceau. I put them in my bike basket and made up for the delay by pedaling faster.

A bunch of pink peonies for the stranger who had put me back on track.

13.

Okay, okay, okay . . . so according to my thirdhand information—it was like a game of telephone, the most random and least reliable method of communication on earth—he, the guy, hadn't said "*at* five o'clock"; he'd said "at *around* five o'clock." I tried to keep that in mind, since it was already past 5:30 and my flowers were starting to wilt.

I didn't recognize any of the servers, and I couldn't keep myself from coming up with a worst-case scenario: no one was ever going to come; it was all a practical joke, a hoax; some pervert's revenge or maybe a new attempt by my dad to humiliate me. Or the evil stepsisters' first act of retaliation.

Someone was making a fool out of me. I was being punished for being so frivolous and then so gullible. All my castles in the sky were being smashed. Everything was rigged against me. Again. Someone had left a negative comment on my wall. I'd been tagged. My website and forums had been hacked. Some fucking troll had taken my bag and my IDs and my things and my roommates' cash, and my last few illusions about life along with it. Or he . . .

I tried to calm down. Maybe he was just late. Or there'd just been a misunderstanding, and we were supposed to meet on Wednesday instead of Tuesday. Or maybe Tuesday of next week?

I sat down anyway, in the same place as the other day, and behaved myself. At first I acted natural—as in, I read a romance novel and waited for some intruder to startle me out of my reverie with an "Ahem," embarrassed but there. But I couldn't stick to my Sleeping Beauty role; I found it impossible to sit still, and stared desperately at the front door looking ugly and Photoshopped and pathetic.

I jumped every time someone passed me, and sighed when they ignored me. Fifteen more minutes and I'd try to call Pauline again. Not my dad, though. He could go to hell.

One waiter who was a little more attentive than the others finally noticed my frenetic fidgeting.

"Are you looking for the restrooms?"

"N—no," I babbled. "I'm meeting . . . I mean, I'm waiting for someone who . . . "

"The purse, right?"

I could have kissed the big idiot right on the mouth. He must have sensed that, because he looked slightly uncomfortable.

"Um . . . he . . . he left already, right?"

He leaned against a column to my left, bent forward slightly, and addressed an invisible bench seat hidden on the other side. "Hey, Romeo. Wake up; your chick is here."

I turned very slowly. Not because I was intimidated, but because I was horribly embarrassed—mortified, even—by the realization that he had been so close to me for so long.

He must have been sitting in the same spot the other time too, hidden in the shadows. That seemed kind of uncool, actually. It's bad manners to hide from ladies, young man.

I turned very slowly because it suddenly occurred to me what he might have—must have—overheard the other day. My meeting with my roommate; her "discreet" envelope; her complaints about my big mouth. The way I'd politely reassured her and then made fun of her two minutes later, imitating her on the phone to Marion. And . . . oh God . . . the telephone. All the hookups and one-night stands and the snickering about crabs. And . . . my panties. And the blow jobs. Oh God. Help.

I turned, gritting my teeth and looking around for some hole I could crawl into and hide before he woke all the way up.

But he was still asleep. Wait, no; he wasn't. Because he was smiling.

He was smiling with his eyes closed. Like a cat. A big tom-cat, up to no good and happy about it.

The Cheshire Cat, straight out of *Mathilde in Fuckupland.*

"See? He was right here! Well, I'll leave you two alone, okay?" said the waiter, edging away.

Gulp.

14.

After a few seconds that seemed to last forever (but which gave me enough time to think *Well shit foiled again he's ugly and fat he has a cowlick he's dressed like a redneck he shaved just before coming here and he cut himself twice he bites his nails he smells weird and I don't see my bag*), he opened his eyes.

He looked at me in a really strange way, as if he were taking aim at me, or secretly challenging me. Then he rubbed his eyes, pulled out an eyelash, and closed his eyes again.

For fuck's sake, I thought. He isn't just ugly; he's drunk too. Or he just smoked some pot. Yeah, that's it. He's totally stoned, the loser.

I leaned over quietly to see if my bag was by his feet, in which case I would grab it and get the hell out of there as fast as I could, leaving him to his leafy pleasures. But no, nothing but a pair of filthy black loafers with round toes, like police shoes, and striped white gym socks.

Oh, girlie.

How have you sunk to this?

Well, I wasn't going to stick around to watch him crash out while I counted his scratches. I turned and picked up my book, waiting for my . . . what did I call him? "Unexpected"? "Heaven-sent"? . . . date to deign to acknowledge me.

Ten minutes went by and I was still reading the same line of text.

I must be losing my mind. What was I doing there? Who had I been waiting for? Who was this guy screwing around with me?

I put down my book and picked up the flowers. I was out of there.

"Mathilde?"

Then, very distinctly:

"Mathilde . . . Edmée . . . Renée . . . Françoise?"

My ears pricked up. I quirked an eyebrow.

"Can I buy you a drink, ladies?"

A comedian. Just my luck.

Well, at least I knew he'd actually had my ID in his hands. That was something, anyway.

When I didn't respond, he unzipped his jacket and I saw my bag against his chest. He didn't say anything else; just put both hands flat on the table and stared at them, then lifted his chin and looked me straight in the eyes:

"Sorry; I got up really early this morning. Are you coming?"

15.

I sat down across from him.

We had a staring contest that lasted about a minute, and I lost. "Were you there on Friday?" I asked.

"Yeah."

"Were you sleeping?"

"No."

"Did I wake you up?"

"Are those flowers for me? That was nice of you."

He took the bouquet out of my hands and held out my bag in return. It was warm. I hugged it to my chest . . . and came alive again.

My own instinct, and everything about him—his weight and his homely face and his smile, and the little cut that was like a brown comma just under his right ear, and his dumb sense of humor and the way he politely hid his yawns behind his big catcher's mitt of a hand—told me, without a doubt, that he hadn't stolen anything from me. And at the same time I was thinking that, I also realized that I wasn't thinking about the envelope, but about all the rest. About me. My deeper self, my trust in mankind. All the punches I'd taken on the chin at an age people think of as innocent, which had shaken me up but not disfigured me.

"What do you want to drink?"

After he'd placed the order we stared at each other silently again like a couple of china figurines.

If we'd been a couple of virginal Mormons having contact for the first time, it would have been positively torrid. After a moment I ventured, awkwardly:

"Is your name really Romeo?"

"No."

"Oh."

"It's Jean-Baptiste."

"Oh."

"Are you disappointed?"

"No."

Talk about snappy dialogue.

I thought about paintings I'd seen of Saint Jean-Baptiste—or rather, of his head on a silver platter, and I saw *him*. All he was missing was a sprig of parsley in each nostril.

The thought made crazy laughter bubble up inside me. I forced it down and managed to keep it to a mere smile—and not a moment too soon. The fact that such an ordinary guy had unsettled me this much annoyed me.

"Are you so happy because you've got your bag back?"

"Yes." I kept smiling.

Our drinks arrived; a tea for me (my good resolutions) and, for him, a double espresso into which he carefully stirred two or three lumps of sugar. Maybe four.

"Do you need to build up your strength?"

"Yeah."

We drank in silence.

He looked at me.

He looked at me for so long that it started to bother me.

"Do I remind you of someone?"

"Yeah."

Okay . . .

Bloody hell, this date was a lot of work. And I didn't particularly want to make conversation with him at all. I was uncomfortable; I felt like he was memorizing me, and his inappropriately studious expression made him look idiotic. I was actually starting to wonder if he might be a little . . . you know, rough around the edges. As in . . . delayed. Removed from the mold too soon. His mouth hung open slightly, and I expected him to start drooling any minute.

God knows I tried, anyway—the air was crisp; Paris was big; the tourists were everywhere; the pigeons were flapping . . . I gave him plenty of decent opportunities to have a conversation, but he wasn't even listening to me. He was lost in silent ecstasy somewhere, and I felt a little like the holy grotto of Lourdes, minus the Virgin and the rosary.

Boy, good thing I'd put on my pretty lingerie, right?

I don't know what finally snapped him out of his daze, but all of a sudden he shook himself, glanced at his watch, and groped for his wallet.

"I have to go."

I didn't say anything. I was relieved. But then, I had to make sure I hadn't been wrong. I love humanity and all, but I'm slightly careful anyway, just out of habit. He must have read my mind, because he looked at me differently just then, with a kind of . . . contempt.

"See that briefcase?"

I hadn't noticed it actually, but sure enough, a slim, pale case stood next to his right leg.

"Look." He indicated a thin chain connecting the handle of the briefcase to one of his belt loops. "There's nothing as valuable in there as what's in your bag, but well, for me it's worth a few months of my salary anyway . . . "

He was quiet. I thought he'd lost his train of thought somewhere along the way, and I was going to say something stupid to ease the tension, but then he said, very softly, fiddling with the chain's links:

"See, Mathilde . . . if you really care about something in life, do whatever it takes not to lose it."

Wait a minute . . . what kind of nutjob had I gotten myself mixed up with here? A lunatic? A preacher's son? A Jehovah's Witness disguised as a country bumpkin, with a briefcase stuffed with apocalyptic tracts and ridiculous prayers?

Of course I was dying to know what he was carrying that was so precious, but knowing that would have been way too good for his ego, and . . . and why was he talking to me like we were best friends, anyway?

"Can you guess what this is?"

Oh God. Help. The game was on. Cape, accessories, and everything.

"A pillow?"

He didn't laugh. Or maybe he hadn't heard me. He put the briefcase on the table, twiddled a code, and turned it to face me, opening the lid.

Now *that*, I hadn't been expecting. He closed the case and stood up.

How can I say this? That big, baby-faced guy with the cow-like expression and the limited vocabulary was walking around with a briefcase full of knives.

He was Rambo. I just hadn't recognized him.

He was already at the bar, paying our tab.

Christ. I got up too.

All of this was well and good, but I wanted to count my damn money!

He held the door open for me and blocked it just as I ducked under his arm. Not for long; half a second, or a quarter of a half-second; just long enough to pretend he'd tripped over his shoelaces and lost his balance and stumbled slightly against the nape of my neck. Barely. Hardly for a second. In the time it took me to be offended we were already outside. But I'd felt the luke-warm tip of his nose against the bone jutting out at the very top of my spine.

I was too anxious to be done with the whole thing to bother telling him off, and disentangled myself quickly.

No coy little games with a guy as gullible as this one. Good riddance to him and his fucking knives. Back to the jungle with you, Cheetah, bye-bye.

Still, I didn't want to leave him on a bad note. He'd never know it, but I owed him a lot.

So buck up, little Madonna of the world's losers; buck up. Say cheese to the nice man. A few nice last words to finish this up; it won't kill you.

"Your jacket," I said. "It has an unusual scent."

"It's deer. Deerskin."

"Oh! Really! I didn't recognize it. Well, um . . . so, good-bye, and thanks again."

I stuck out my hand. The problem was that he wouldn't give it back.

"Uh . . . I . . . I mean, uh . . . I'd like to see you again."

I laughed loudly, to make sure I'd get rid of him for good, and then said: "Something tells me you've got my number already."

But even as I was saying the words, I was thinking how fake it sounded, my bitchy little laugh.

"N—no," he stammered, looking at my arm.

He'd suddenly gone pale.

Pale, serious, helpless, and sad. His face looked ten years

older. He looked up and, for the first time, I had the feeling that he was seeing *me*.

"I had it all, of course, but I . . . I've got nothing now, because I . . . I gave you everything."

Ooo-kay. I wondered if he was about to break out his violin. He seemed sincere, but come on, he was laying it on a bit thick, right?

Panic kicked in in my head: *Oh Christ, do* not *give him your number. He's obviously completely out of his mind. Yes, he is! Look. Look at him! Look at his face; he's like Jack the Ripper's country cousin! And besides, you may not have noticed, but he's missing the tip of a finger. And he's fat, too. And I mean, fine, he's honest, I'm not saying he isn't, but he's seriously ugly. You tend to attract nothing but pains in the ass, which you know all too well. You've already given out your number a million times. Come on, Mathilde, lie. Yes, you can! Just lie about the last digit, then. It won't be the first time or the last.*

I know, but . . . he's been really classy about this whole thing.

What the hell do you know about him, idiot? You haven't even opened your fucking bag!

Maybe not, but at least I have it. I'm not off crying for my mother at the police station right now.

I could always give it to him and not answer when he calls . . .

Fine, do whatever you want, but really, you're asking for it, you know?

It's true that I'd had my share of sad stories recently. I don't know if it was some old dispute between Cupid and me, but how much damage could he do to me with this chubby four-eyes? Never mind, go on. I'd give him my number for one reason, and one only: I was afraid he might have kept my father's number and would call him out of desperation. If it came down to a choice between the old head case and this new one, I'd rather deal with the latter.

"Um . . . could you let my hand go for a second?"

He had squeezed it so hard that the redness of his big fingers had rubbed off on mine.

I wrote my number down on a metro ticket. He looked at it for a long time, as if reassuring himself that it was valid, then slid it into the depths of his wallet, which he tucked into the inside pocket of his jacket. He gazed at me one last time, nodded, and took off in the opposite direction.

Phew.

I took three steps before turning around; I was confused, truthfully, about all the bad thoughts that had been swirling around in my head.

"Hey . . . uh . . . Jean-Baptiste!"

He turned.

"Thank you!"

Last look, last smile—much more tight-lipped than the others. Last shrug of the shoulders, which could mean "It was nothing," "Shut the hell up," or "Piss off," and he was off again.

I watched him in the distance, crossing the Avenue de Friedland with his deerskin-covered back slightly hunched over, his huge knives in one hand and his bunch of peonies in the other, and I was . . . disturbed.

The proof of that? I waited until I was at home before opening my bag and finally counting my cash.

16.

It was all there. So was the money in my wallet. For some reason I neither understood nor liked, I found myself a bit disappointed.

I changed into jeans, added my five thousand bucks to the damned envelope, left it on the kitchen table with a little note that basically said: "Here you go, and now leave me alone about your fucking remodeling," and then I was out the door.

My precious little princesses would be back any minute, and that was more than I could handle. Marion too. All of it. Everything had become more than I could handle.

I still felt like crying, so I went to the movies and saw a romantic comedy.

ACT TWO

1.

The end credits had barely started—I wasn't going to tell this part, but what the hell, at this point it's probably not worth it to try to make myself look good—when I took out my phone, hoping he'd called.

Hoping *he* had called. Jean-Baptiste the Warrior.

Of course, at the time, I would have sworn up and down that that wasn't true, no, really, blah blah blah, but if I look back honestly at the dishonest girl walking back up the Rue Caulaincourt on that April night, pulling her shabby old duffle coat more closely around her, I can tell you—and you can put it in writing, Madam Court Reporter—that it wasn't the six o'clock movie occupying her thoughts.

It was his face she couldn't stop thinking about. Their conversation (unforgettable) playing in a loop in her head. His sugar lumps she counted again and again while clutching the silent piece of plastic in her pocket.

* * *

And then? Then, life went back to normal.

That's what people say when nothing happens, right?

When you forget your New Year's resolutions, when you abandon your dreams of freedom (why leave when my room was just repainted?) and greatness (why resume my studies when my computer's raking in money for me like a one-armed bandit?), and when you drink like a fish and run around making up comedies that aren't romantic at all.

Taking Paul's clothes off and putting Pierre's clothes back on and finally ending up naked in Jacques's arms.

Yeah, that's what they say.

That waiting room called youth.

What had my sleepy nutcase become? A joke, an anecdote, a funny story to tell at dinner. It was a hit; I gave him one less finger and one more knife every time I told it. After a while it was like *Lord of War* in a Calcutta leper colony.

I thought about him, in the beginning. There were things about him that still bothered me: the way he'd said, "Are you coming?" in such an authoritative voice; the precise way he'd memorized me from head to toe; how sad he'd seemed when he talked about seeing me again, and the fact that he hadn't had to fumble around so much, when he could have gotten the number from my phone all by himself. And then I saw his white socks again in my head, and turned back to my brother-in-law's webcams feeling freshly inspired.

My trusty GPS was right: dead end, straight ahead.

* * *

Three times over the next few days, someone tried to call me in the middle of the night but didn't leave a message. The first time I thought it was a mistake; the second, I had my doubts, and the last time I knew it was him. I recognized his silence.

It was two o'clock in the morning but I was still awake; I tried to call him back but the number was a landline somewhere in Île-de-France, and the rings died away in the distance.

That was when something started to come unhinged inside

me. I went against one of my few principles (both moral and "health-related," if you know what I mean) and slept with my phone turned on next to my pillow. Too bad about the radiation, too bad about cancer, and too bad about my pride and my getting any sleep; I needed to be sure. Who was calling me so furtively, as if they were trying to make sure I wouldn't pick up? Who? And if it was him, why? What did he want from me, really? At the time I didn't think at all about the . . . I don't know . . . the significance of an act like that, and yet . . . what better way to insinuate yourself into someone else's private life than by interfering with their sleep?

From then on, every night, I turned up my ringer to its maximum volume and shared my bed with a phantom.

I went out less. Yeah, it kills me to admit it, and I had a thousand reasons ready for anyone who might act curious about it, but the simple fact was that I went out less. Ten days—or rather, ten nights—had passed without a hitch, and I'd decided to turn off my mobile phone because I wasn't sleeping well. I woke up from time to time to see if the little "missed call" signal was blinking, or to make sure my telephone hadn't been suffocated by the duvet.

And I was angry at him. And angry at myself, really angry, for having become such a flake. I was so angry at both of us that I remember going to bed that night promising myself it would be the last time. His last chance to come back to haunt me.

He could go right to hell with his chains and his knives and his sneaky calls. I was tired of this crap.

Phones, text messages, screens, chats, and e-mails . . . I didn't want these imaginary borders on my map of Tendre anymore.

I'd given; I'd suffered; I'd paid for my share of all these half-assed, absurd, naïve plans imposed on us by love in the digital age.

Yes. I was tired. Even worse, I felt worn down, emptied out, disembodied by loving so many times without really loving. Now I wanted real experiences with real people who had real flesh on their bones. Otherwise, I'd prefer to skip my turn.

And because he's very strong, and when it comes to fat he's right there, you know; that night, he called back.

2.

He must have called earlier than the other times, because I was in the middle of that first deep sleep, and at first I couldn't figure out if it was in a dream or reality that I stuck out an arm and felt some smooth, hard, slightly warm object against my ear.

Nothing happened. It was a dream.

"Jean-Baptiste?" I murmured groggily.

" . . . "

"Is it you?"

"Yes."

"The other times, too?"

" . . . "

"Why are you doing that? Why aren't you talking?"

" . . . "

I was curled around the phone in my hand. A long time went by. Much too long. I fell asleep waiting for him to answer.

I don't know how many minutes went by. In the morning my call log would say that our conversation lasted two hours and thirty-four minutes, but I think I must not have hung up correctly. Finally I heard:

"Mmmffrffmmteet."

I opened my eyes, and this time it was my turn to be silent.

"Are you still there?" he asked anxiously.

"Yeah."

"I'm . . . I'm a chef, you see."

" . . . "

" . . . and I'd like to have you over for something to eat."

Ohh. Okay. I'd thought he was saying something about fixing his heat. I mean, what bizarre parallel dimension had we fallen into? A weird, inhibited, insomniac chef calling me at twelve-fifteen in the morning to read me his menu? Go back to sleep, kiddies! Everything's under control! Don't let the bedbugs bite!

"Would you like to?"

"Now??"

"No." His voice sounded happier. "I have to prepare!"

"When?"

"I'll let you know. I need to get organized. Can you write down a phone number and call me back tomorrow night at the same time?"

What a practical schedule.

"Go ahead; I'm listening."

I grabbed a book at random from my bedside table. Still half-asleep, by the light of my phone's screen, I wrote down the string of numbers he dictated. After that, I don't know. I heard my first name one or two more times, but I'll never know if it was his voice or its echo in my sleep-fogged mind.

3.

In the morning I knew it hadn't been a dream, because a telephone number was scribbled on the inside cover page—oh, irony—of Michael Connelly's *The Scarecrow*.

The problem was that I must have really been out of it, because I couldn't read my own handwriting. Was that a 7, or a 3, or a 1? And was that a 2, a 3, or a 5?

Fine, I'd try them all.

I was useless at math and even worse at calculating probabilities, but I could already tell that this little puzzle was going to take a while to solve.

The other problem was there was no reasonable way I could wait until midnight to try a whole bunch of possible wrong numbers. I'd wake up all kinds of nice people and possibly get lynched in the process. So I started dialing at around ten o'clock, and good thing, because two hours later I still hadn't gotten my guy.

The voices answering the phone got less and less friendly, and I started to lose track of my combinations. I couldn't remember which ones I'd already tried. I just kept asking for Jean-Baptiste and saying, "Oh, excuse me," and apologizing and wreaking havoc in every household in Île-de-France with a telephone number starting with 01.42, 01.43, or 01.45. And finally, well, fuck. I gave up.

This whole thing was messing with my head. He'd call me back.

Obsessives can never let anything go.

I was as on-edge as a person can possibly be. My paperback was covered with crossed-out numbers and my mobile phone was on the verge of imploding.

I went out.

I went to get some air with other, more talkative insomniacs.

I swear, this guy was really starting to make me lose my mind, the head case! He could go fuck himself. He could go cook his crappy food for girls who were in his own league! Besides, I'm no foodie. I don't give a shit about French gastronomy, any more than I do about what I ate as a baby. Give me a crouton and I'm happy.

God, I was a bitch. He'd been obsessed with me even before he started cooking, the asshole.

My nerves were in shreds and my mouth tasted like bile. I needed to hang up, to let go of the prize, to forget all this crap and get on my bike.

Yes, that's what I needed. To go out and dance, and drink, and forget him.

And I pedaled, and pedaled, and pedaled, and went further and further off the rails.

I yelled at the stars.

I said to them: "Why does this shit always happen to me, huh? Yeah, you, Grandpa, up there, I'm talking to you! Why do you only send nutjobs my way? I mean, fuck, it's your job! Well, it's fine. You've already done quite enough for me. Please, God; please, I'm begging you—abandon me."

4.

He never called back.

Not that night, or the ones that followed.

Still, I tortured myself for a few more nights by leaving my phone on—but no. I'd fucked up where he was concerned. He wasn't that crazy.

Or maybe he was a lot crazier. Or less keen than I'd thought.

He'd been a pain in the ass from beginning to end, the tub of lard.

And life—how did I put it again?—"went back to normal." There you have it.

Shit.

5.

I got over it, of course. I'd been through worse things than that, as they say. It was springtime. Springtime in Paris; the springtime of Cole Porter and Ella Fitzgerald. Terraces and promises and the days stretched out in front of me; I was alive and in good health; I had other advantages and more than one trick to pull out of my sleeve.

I'm serious. I'd forgotten him. And then, one morning, I emptied out my bag, because I wanted to switch to a different one. Because I was going to a wedding and I needed something cuter. And that day, chef's surprise: *bombe glacée* and chicken in mustard sauce.

My chef popped up without warning, and I was caught unawares at the buffet.

Sticky patch ahead. Very sticky.

ASIDE

1.

If I had an archenemy and wanted to inflict the worst torture on her, the gentlest, the slowest, the cruelest and most disfiguring, I'd push her into the arms of a writer; I'd wait for her to fall in love, the purest love, and then I'd watch her suffer as I flipped carelessly through an old issue of *Vogue*.

I was barely nineteen when that catastrophe happened to me. Nineteen. A child. And an orphan, on top of that. Good times. Like a bird falling from its empty nest with its big sad eyes and its bald head. With such soft flesh. Straight into a novel. A first novel. Hell of a beautiful thing, and a fucking fantastic subject too, right?

Okay, I'll stop. He's made a name for himself since then. I brought him luck, or maybe my circumstances did, and he doesn't need any publicity. He's done very well in that department all by himself. Someday, when I'm really old, someone might ask me a question or two for a footnote, but in the meantime I'd rather stay silent.

Peace.

Peace to artists.

Peace to myths.

Just one last thing, though. The passing of this guy, this man, this thief through my life had only one real effect in the end: to remind me, and comfort me in the certainty that my mother's long illness and suffering had given me, a few years earlier, that the expression "That which doesn't kill us makes us stronger" is complete crap. That which doesn't kill you, doesn't kill you. Period.

(That was a really complicated and probably grammatically incorrect sentence, which I can easily simplify as follows: that bastard fucked me up, big time.)

My turn, Master Boileau.

* * *

He was my first love. It wasn't the first time I'd slept with a man, but it was the first time I'd made love, and it was . . . well, I said I'd stop, and I will. I'm no writer, and I certainly don't need to torture myself with the past, or put my emotions in test tubes and refine what I went through into crystalline form to make stones I can throw . . . so keep it brief, Mathilde, keep it brief. Don't ruin the last tiny shred of dignity he was kind enough (or negligent enough) to leave you with, please.

Okay, okay. We'll put an ellipse there. (Ha ha, yes, he did teach me one or two things along the way . . .) Let's just say, for the purposes of this story, that this lovely person had sent me tons of letters—love letters, as I proudly thought at the time, but which I have since had to admit were lyrics and writing exercises—that I eventually threw away one night when I thought I was free of him.

Yep, I ended up buried under a heap of cigarette butts, empty bottles, coffee grounds, and dirty makeup-remover pads.

Hallelujah. I'd finally gotten rid of the letters.

Except for one.

Oh, really? Why?

Why that one?

Because it was the last one. Because it belonged to me more than all the others. Because I was, and still am, weak enough to think that it was sincere, and even if it hadn't been, that didn't matter much anymore. I'm honest enough to distinguish between the beautiful and the true, and to choose the beautiful when it's obvious. Because the question of figuring out whether something is art or smut has never really interested me. Because that letter reminded me that I'd been loved by a talented guy, that I'd inspired him, and that yes, despite everything, despite him, I'd been that lucky.

And because it's beautiful.
And I was beautiful, too.

Because I grew up with it. Because it watched me grow up. Just ordinary sheets of A4 paper, but loaded with little marks in black ink and placed in a series by which I was first horribly embarrassed then flattered, skeptical, nauseated, prostrate with sorrow and huddled over a wastebasket, and finally . . . changed.

Changed. Fatalistic. Conservative. Guarded. The guardian of the little temple of what served as my life before ending up in . . .

. . . my handbag.

Out of discretion. So it wouldn't fall into the hands of my roommates or anyone else. Ever.

It was in the little pocket hidden in the inner lining. The only one that closed with a zipper. Narrow, discreet, undetectable by anyone who wasn't specifically looking for it.

It was still there, but it wasn't in its envelope anymore as I was sure I'd put it in, but around the envelope instead. Clamping down around my name and my address at the time—as if telling me, I imagine, that it had been read and that it was important for me to know that.

(Oh, stupid language! Not there; not now! Not at this exact moment in my story! And I laugh. All alone, and loudly, at being subjected to such ridiculous rules of agreement.)

... and that it was important for me to be informed of that. There. It's a more awkward way of saying it, but it'll do.

* * *

Yes, you see, I asked a stranger to address the envelope for me. A clumsy fake-out, I know, but don't send it back to me. Not this letter. It's more worthy than I am, I promise.
If you don't want to read it now, then wait. Wait two months, or two years, or maybe ten years. Wait until you don't care anymore.
Ten years. I really think highly of myself.
Wait as long as you need to, but one day, please, unfold it. Please.

Our last conversation—or our final battle, should I say—has been haunting me for weeks. You chastised me for my egotism, my vileness, my selfishness. You accused me of using you, sucking you dry, loving what you inspired in me instead of who you were.
You said I'd never loved you.

You feel betrayed. You threw it in my face that you'd never read another book as long as you live. You said you hated words as much as you hated me and even more, if that kind of repulsion was humanly possible. That words were pathetic weapons in the hands of pathetic people like me. That they were worthless, they said nothing, they lied. That they destroyed everything they touched, and that I'd made you permanently disgusted by them.

Now, tonight, in two months or in two years, you'll read the words below and you'll know, my love, that you weren't always right.

Your closed eyelids when you fell asleep in my arms, Mathilde, looked like the insides of lychee husks. The same iridescent gleam, the same pink, unexpected and poignant. Your pretty earlobes were like two plump coxcombs—tiny porcelain pebbles, made tender and meltingly soft from simmering so long in a broth of saliva from your endless frothy kisses—and their spiraling cartilage teases, like Carême's beignets, a fricassee of birds' heads.

The scent of your hair, there where it grows at the back of your neck, just above that delta, that secret downy gap, that funnel for caresses, had the piquant bitterness of the inside of a loaf of bread, and your fingernails—to someone who spent hours sucking them—were like so many almonds blanched a bit too early before summer's end.

The hollow between your collarbones sparkled with a tangy juice that fizzed on the tongue, and the curve of your shoulder provided the fresh, fine-grained flesh, meltingly soft as the bottom of a pear, to soothe it.

An Anjou pear suckled in the shadowy light of the saddler . . .

At the corner of your mouth, those minuscule bubbles of saliva when you laughed sparkled like drops of pink champagne, and the tip of your tongue, my beloved, had the grain, the dusky red, the pale and delicate roughness of wild strawberries.

The same adorable, innocent, hidden sweetness, secret, shy, and desperately, desperately sweet.

Your nipples? Two little Provence beans, the first ones, the ones gathered in February, which must be earned, shucked while raw, and the curves of your breasts beneath my hands had the smooth golden softness of spring butter.

The little valleys leading to your belly button, if I moistened you with pleasure, had the sweet tang of wild plums picked in forgotten hedgerows and happily awakened a mouth heavy with so much sweetness.

Your hips were like two beautiful brioche tops, and the small of your back had—always, I imagine—no, I remember—the delicate taste of acacia blossoms. A heady, imperious fragrance that continued along the curves of your buttocks until the exquisite creases where your thighs met. That tender, dimpled flesh, soft and shining, which so often imprisoned overly daring fingers . . .

The arches of your feet were musky, the hollows of your ankles bitter, the lengths of your calves fruity, the backs of your knees salty. The insides of your thighs tasted mineral, and what ran between them, and what came next, and what dripped at the end, was a reduction of everything that had led me there. A core. The core of you and of the whole universe.

That taste, the taste of your being, modern-day princess, delicious, unseemly, and tattooed, to which I helped myself then and overindulged in . . . well, now I have only words with which to savor it.
Alas, these miserable tools—and it's you who reminded me of this—they're worthless. They know nothing, invent nothing, and teach nothing when they remember, and relate the tale . . .
More than your skin, your hair, your fingernails or your scent, it's your essence, your humors, the lifeblood of your insides, your pectin, your vaginal juices—that messenger, elevator operator, telltale of your hunger, your thirst, and your giddiness—that altar boy of your desires—that still, even tonight, makes my mouth water.

"What did she taste like, your beloved?" ask all 26 letters of the only alphabet I ever learned, "and what order would you put us in, if you challenged us to tell her?"
Swallow's nest. Warm fig. Overripe apricot. Tiny raspberry swallowed beneath an icy drizzle.
Sometimes, wood shavings. Sometimes, tides, soul blood

and menstrual blood. Or soft roe. Or milkiness. Aphrodite's colostrum.
A terrifying mixture of mother's milk and the snot of an animal in heat.

Truffle in aspic. Bouquet garni of labias and hems of flesh poached to moistness. Eviscerated stingray. Pink flesh attached to a fish bone. The water from shellfish. The juice beneath the shells. Emulsion of sea-urchin coral. Suction of ink from jig-boat-fished calamari. Crazy calisthenics. Pussy against the flat of my tongue. Ambrosial candy. Citron. The iodine-tinged zest of a red grapefruit. Vi . . .
Oh, Mathilde.
I give up.

I loved you.

I loved you more than I can say.
And much less well.

2.

My hands shook. Something—I don't know exactly what; lingering shame, modesty, secrets torn open, deflowered—rose up in my throat, turning my stomach on the way.

I didn't understand what was happening to me. *Hey now, you're getting all worked up. Calm down, old girl, calm down.* It's nothing, it *was* nothing, just a little highbrow wank job by a nerd telling himself a story while he sucked himself off.

Plus he couldn't even pass the qualification test in cutlery and charcuterie.

Doesn't matter. I burned it in the sink straightaway.

I was shaking and sweating. I was nauseated. I put great effort into pushing the little shreds of blackened paper toward the drain, one hand cupped over my mouth.

I was rushing, I was ready, I was late. Cold sweat stung my face and I felt my makeup streaming off in rivulets.

I threw up.

3.

I scrubbed the sink out with Javel and rinsed it copiously with water. For a long time. Meticulously. It was time for all that misery to disappear into the sewers of Paris.

"Are you okay?"

Pauline's voice.

I hadn't heard her come through the front door. It wasn't my health that was worrying her; it was the waste of water.

"Are you sick?"

I turned around to reassure her, and I could see that she didn't believe me.

"My God! What's happened to you now? Did you drink too much last night? Is that it?"

What a reputation.

"No!" I babbled stupidly, trying to fix my mascara with an index finger. "It's just, tonight—tonight is a big night—I look chic, right? I'm going to my friend Charlotte's wedding . . . "

She didn't smile. "Mathilde?"

"Yes?"

"I don't understand the way you're living your life . . . "

"I don't either!" I laughed, wiping my nose with the back of my hand.

She shrugged and headed for her beloved kettle.

I felt stupid. It was rare for her to take an interest in me like that. I wanted to make amends. And I needed to confide in someone.

"Do you remember . . . the guy who found my bag?"

"The weirdo?"

"Yeah."

"Have you heard from him again? Is he bothering you? Oh, damn, there's hardly any tea left . . . "

"No."

"I'll have to tell Julie to get some more."

"He's a chef."

She looked at me strangely. "Oh . . . oh, really? So what? Why are you telling me this?"

"I just . . . look, I'm going out, otherwise I'll just screw everything up again."

"When will you be home?"

"I don't know."

She followed me to the door. "Mathilde?"

"Yes."

She straightened my collar. "You look pretty."

I smiled at her, bowing my head piously.

She thought I was charmingly embarrassed, but really I was fighting back tears.

4.

Then . . . nothing. Then is now, and I have nothing left to tell. Plus I don't even want to anymore. Now, and even if you can't tell with the naked eye, I'm curled up on the edge of life and I'm just waiting for it to go by.

Latent depression. I can't remember where I picked up that two-faced rat of an expression, but I used it again with pleasure. It suited me. The latent part, I suppose. For years people had cited me as an example of it, put it into my head even with my strength, my cheerfulness, my courage, and . . . well, it was only too easy for them, the cowards. Much too easy. It's true that I've tried to protect you, and held on as long as I could, but I can't go on with it anymore.

I'm exhausted.

Because it was all an act, my friends. Oh yes, all of it. All of it was just an act. I knew that my mother was filling out those testing form thingies any which way, checking boxes wherever she had to. She'd leave them lying around on purpose, to reassure me. I knew that all the good news she spent hours talking loudly on the phone to my grandmother about was nothing but hot air. I knew they were both lying to me. I knew my father went straight off to fuck his whore after he dropped my mom off at the hospital for her chemo, and I knew she knew it too.

I knew he'd be out of the house even before her body was cold. That I'd end up living with my older sister, that I'd shave my head and my eyebrows, that I'd fail my high school exams and babysit my sister's kids to earn my keep. I knew I'd act sweet, classy, above suspicion; that I'd be Auntie Yoyo, who jumped on the beds and knew how to arrange the Pokémon and Bella Sara cards perfectly. I knew I'd let my hair grow back. That I'd make up for lost time, sleep around like crazy, drink like a fish. That I'd build a reputation for myself as a major party girl, tough and always up for anything, so that people would label me as they should, and write me off for good when they did.

I knew that my brother-in-law worked me as hard as he did so he could pretend to be Mickey Corleone, that family was sacred and blah blah blah, but I also knew that if I stopped doing his dirty work, someone else would come along in my place and do it just as well. Yeah, I *knew* all that, and if I never told you anything it's because I'm generous.

The only thing I found beautiful during all those years spent at the front—the only time I didn't lie—an asshole turned it into a book. So there you go. It might be polite to be happy, as they say, but today I don't care about being polite anymore.

Today I am flat on my back. I'm sticking out my middle finger and pulling the plug.

But, unfortunately, you can't fight your own nature, so— good girl that I am—I'm going to finish out this story. I'm warning you, though: you can push fast-forward a few times. You won't miss much.

1.

O ne day, once upon a time, I forgot my handbag in a café near the Arc de Triomphe. In that bag there was an unsealed envelope containing a hundred 100-euro bills. A hundred green bills straight from the bank. Nice and crisp, well-ironed and clean as new money. A big guy found it and gave it back to me four days later, intact.

Carefully hidden inside that bag, there was also a letter that told the life story of my cunt and my tits in 3-D. These things happen, I guess. Maybe not quite as juicy a letter as that, but photos, videos, compromising texts, indiscreet attachments; seductive, disgusting, and malicious pixels. With all these snitching thinga-majigs, all this paraphernalia of narcissism and shamelessness we're all so determined to equip ourselves with in this day and age, some major heartache is bound to result, don't you think?

Oh yes, it is. There's no way these things won't pour salt in wounds and on shredded hearts. So why was I taking it so badly? Why was I acting like a freaked-out virgin all of a sudden? Why should it matter to me that a guy I was never going to see again had gotten a little taste of me? My squawking didn't make sense. When had I become so delicate? Fucking hell. I felt it anyway.

Nothing made sense anymore, least of all me.

I went to that wedding with two Spasfon tablets under my tongue and the certainty that I'd end up torpedoed. I might have looked pretty, but it wouldn't last. I could depend on that.

2.

I arrived out of breath and, in my mandatory killer stilettos, I twisted my ankle running headlong up the front steps of the 20th Arrondissement courthouse.

Grimacing, I caught up with a guy who was as dressed up as I was, though he seemed to be in much less of a hurry. "Excuse me, you . . . uh . . . I . . . I'm looking for the wedding hall . . . do you know where it is?"

He offered an arm for me to lean on while I got my glass slipper back on, then said in a very friendly way:

"The funny farm? It's over there! I'm in too—going to the ceremony, I mean. Stick with me, wobbly one, we'll be less conspicuous that way."

Bingo; I'd found my second thief. He was probably the one who put me in a taxi sometime well after midnight; I'd lost my shoes hours ago.

The newlyweds never called me again, or thanked me for my wedding gift. I don't remember what state I was in, let alone what I might have said to their guests, but it must not have been very nuptial.

3.

B ut that was the last time I got plastered.
And because they don't seem like much, those six virtu-
ous little words all lined up in a row: the-last-time-I-got-
plastered, I wasn't suspicious of them.

Big mistake.

It was a very bad sign.

Because what's left for people who have stopped drinking,
even though they were using it as a last refuge against despair?

Despair.

It was all muddled. It's a muddle, despair. Especially in my
case, as a three-card trick player who'd known how to mix it
all up so well for so many years.

I had trouble distinguishing overindulgence from actual suffering, and since I'm much too cowardly to lift up my big rock
and try to understand what's swarming around under it, I'll
stick to the symptoms—the external signs of distress. Yes, I'd
stopped drinking, but I wasn't eating either, and I could barely
sleep. That was a lot of unpleasantness for simple overindulgence, you have to admit.

Someone else, someone braver or smarter or less of a
cheapskate, would have gone in for a consultation. Maybe not
a psychiatrist right away, but at least a doctor, the good family doctor she no longer had, or any old GP in her neighborhood, and without going into detail, she would have said up
front: Hi Doctor, everything's fine, really really fine, I swear,

but I have to get some sleep, do you understand? I have to sleep at least a little, or I'm going to keel over. Oh, my appetite, that's no big deal. I have hips like nice big brioche tops. And plus, look, I'm up to almost two packs of Marlboros a day, that's plenty. But the nights . . . the nights, all of them, always, always totally sleepless . . . that'll kill you in the end, right?

That's exactly what I was in the middle of brooding about at the very beginning of this story, when I was dragging myself from the Place de l'Étoile to the Montmartre cemetery in the middle of the night, stuffing a seventh unsuccessful receipt into my pocket.

Yep. I'm not very clever. It took all of that to bring us here. The starting point.

What?

Seven?!?

But—but, Mathilde—you just turned over all three of your cards at once! You've had it, my dear! You're lost! Do you know what the three-card trick is called in English? Find the Lady. And that's it? That's what your queen of hearts was hiding? You're letting that fatso get you in such a state?

. . .

With his patent-leather shoes and the gym socks with the reinforced toes?

. . .

And his missing finger? And the sharp knives chained to his pants?

. . .

And his jacket that stinks of goat?

. . .

And his nocturnal whims?

. . .

Let me remind you that he still has your number. You may

be too hopeless to write a phone number down legibly, but he could have called you back eventually, if he'd wanted to.

. . .

Well, maybe not. I mean, with only nine fingers, maybe he couldn't manage it . . .

. . .

Yo, Mathilde! You should answer when someone speaks to you!

Shut up. Make fun of me, taunt me, put me down as much as you want, but don't reprimand me. Don't tell me the lesson. You know how much I hate that. If you persist in that tone you're going to lose me completely. So . . . so what do you want me to tell you, then?

Everything, gorgeous.
Everything.
Get comfortable and have a seat.

4.

So . . . um . . . where should I start? And where am I, first of all?

Boulevard de Courcelles. Okay. I have time.

I regretted burning my letter. I regretted burning it without rereading it one last time. I couldn't remember exactly what sweet talk he'd used, and the way it rambled about me distorted things. I regretted not cleansing my palate one last time, imagining myself a little bit the way he thought of me, remembering the state of my arsenal.

I started off at a disadvantage. I would have liked to know just as much about him as he did about me. Well . . . okay, not exactly that much, but more than I did, at least. More than little cuts from a razor blade, a cowlick, a missing fingertip, a way of staring, and the manners of a hustler.

I felt like I was missing something, and I felt hurt by it.

I wanted to understand how it was possible in this day and age, in the world we live in, this world we've created, this vast casino in which I shamelessly gambled every morning, for one individual to return ten thousand euros in cash to another individual, a complete stranger, without saying anything except a benevolent warning about the importance of not letting one's good fortune get away, and then pay the check at the end of the night on top of it all.

I wanted to understand how it was possible to be tactless enough to rummage through a girl's handbag and leave enough signs that she'd be sure to know it; to force open her innermost private life and then be troubled by that; to let her into the secret again by staring at her deeply, calmly, and silently in the back of a café for more than half an hour, and then to sniff her in the doorway before taking her hand and refusing to give it back— and at the same time to be enough of an idiot to give her back her stuff without having the bright idea of writing down her phone number, making it necessary to ask her for it, and then to call her on the sly at all hours of the night as if it were a capital offense—and yet to have the plan, the need, the desire to over-come all her qualms, and to restore the appetite she had lost, and get her all stirred up without even knowing; to subject her to the disappointment, the very next night, of seeing a rabbit-skin jacket on some big guy with his back turned (not that he knew about that, but how could he?)—and not even to have taken the trouble to call her back, the ungrateful bitch, the fucking liar, the filthy seductress—so he could seduce her in his turn?

In summary, I wanted to know what planet this bizarre guy came from, and if it was Earth, I wanted finally to feel, just a little, what humanity was.

I wanted to let myself starve to death so he would gather me up and tuck me away in the same place he'd kept my mom's purse, the other bastard's tasting menu, and my mess of a life: beneath his jacket.

Yeah. I wanted that, only that. For him to zip up his jacket and let me finally rest against his big chest.

. . .

Aha, that shut you up, didn't it! You're thinking, what is she babbling about now, the stupid girl?

After the poet of my thighs with his starry lute, after that whole horde of good-for-nothings, and before the poor sod who will finally manage to get himself hooked and end up with

three kids crammed in a minivan, she has to have her fantasy of
an assistant chef with his nice big mitts, his houndstooth pants,
and his clunky clogs, is that it?

Gross.

Gross, gross, gross.

That's it. Come at me.

Come at me, losers.

Unload on the white dove.

Isn't Facebook fantasy? And Match.com, and OkCupid, and
Meetup? And all those ridiculous social websites. All those miserable cauldrons where you stir your loneliness in between two
advertisements, all those "likes," all those networks of imaginary
friends, monitored communities, penniless, sheeplike, paying
fraternities connected to wealthy servers . . . what is that?

And that anxiety, that permanent state of missing something,
that empty space beside you, these telephones that you're endlessly messing with, these screens you have to unlock again and
again and again, these lives you buy so you can keep playing,
this wound, this plug, these clenched fists in your pocket? That
way you—all of you—have to keep checking and checking all
the time to see if someone has left you a note, a message, a sign,
a call back, a notification, an advertisement, an . . . an anything.

And that "someone," who could be anyone or anything,
from the moment he (or it) touches you, he reassures you—
reminds you—that you're alive, that you exist, that you count,
and that for want of knowing you otherwise, he might try to
hand you a last little bit of bullshit along the way.

All these depths of despair, all this dizziness, all these lines
of code you toy with on the metro and toss out like so much
old shit as soon as "it" doesn't hold your attention anymore.
All these distractions that distract you from yourself, which
have made you lose the habit of thinking about yourself,

dreaming about yourself, to talk with the deepest part of yourself, to get to know yourself or recognize yourself, to look at other people, to smile at strangers, to make eye contact, to flirt, to make out, and even to fuck—but which give you the illusion of being, and of embracing the whole world . . .

All these coded feelings, all the friendships just hanging by a thread, which have to be recharged every evening, and of which nothing would remain if the fuses blew—that's not fantasy at least, right?

And I know what I'm talking about.

I bleed, too.

I didn't care if he was a chef or a street cleaner or a stockbroker. Even if I am weak enough to believe that, to choose a crappy career that consists of feeding people just like him day after day, he had to be fundamentally good.

I don't see how you can keep going, otherwise.

Maybe there are bad people who wear chef's jackets, but to get up so early and go to bed so late, to be so cold every morning when accepting the food deliveries and then so hot over the stoves, to be under such pressure at the times of intense action that they fall asleep in a café on their breaks, to endure the pain of plunging boiling vegetables into ice-baths so they keep their beautiful colors, and in doing so to give themselves a permanent glowing red face, to feel all greasy even on their days off, but still to have enough energy to tie on an apron and feed their friends and family and their friends' friends—all you people fortunate enough to have a chef nearby and to be happy with him, well, maybe I'm wrong, but I think they have to be good people. Generous, at least. Brave, for sure. Because satiety is an ungrateful thing. So, so ungrateful. You always have to start again.

And admitting that that I'm dabbling in pure fantasy, really, and that for every pure heart there are ten food bureaucrats, ten potato-peelers, ten embittered assholes, ten unqualified people who have passed the professional certification, ten pencil-pushers, ten people who passed the test because there was no one better who will spend the rest of their lives counting their hours worked, their burns, and their potato peels—and being resigned and bitter and as discouraging and discouraged as anyone can legitimately be with a job like that . . . admitting that, well, you know what he would have done about my little fantasy? He would have stolen my ten thousand bucks.

Yes.

Oh, yes.

Am I wrong to bring everything back to money? No, of course not; it's the barometer, and you know it.

And admitting that I was enough of an idiot to dream up this kind of comedy, and to foist it all off on the first pancake-flipper who came along and made the poor choice to nod off behind my back—yes, admitting that too (but Christ, what else am I supposed to think about when I don't have my bike and all the shops are closed?), well, there again, I think he made out pretty well for a poor dumb decent guy, in my opinion.

Because there were enough bombs in that bag to ruin my life. I know, because I'm the one who dropped them all on him.

Cash stolen or not, bag entrusted to a third party or not, he had everything he needed, in the way of information, to have a hell of a good time. To stalk me, and find me, and keep waking me up in the middle of the night, asking me, Woof woof! if it were true that I was too good, if I still liked—heh heh—to chew on crushed ice, if there were still lard in my cleavage, and if my ass—oh la la—really smelled like flowers and mussel juice.

That kind of calling card, in a girl's bag, was outstanding at the bar.

But instead of that he turned pale, promising me, distraught, that he'd "given everything back."

There. That's all.

Boulevard des Batignolles.

Mercy, I haven't gone to bed.

But whatever. There you go. You can just make out the top of my Sacré-Coeur in the distance.

. . .

Still speechless, eh?

. . .

Did I say something to upset you?

. . .

Well?? You should answer when someone speaks to you, too!

It's just . . . I never imagined all of that.

All of what?

Uh, that you were so . . .

So what?

Well, that you were so scrawny. It doesn't show from a distance.

Nothing shows from a distance.

. . .

Believe me. Believe me, because I'm an expert on these things. Each and every one of us keeps most of our life secret. From far away, close up, straight on, in profile, or at an angle, nothing ever shows.

. . .

Come on, say something! Give me a break; talk to me again. I'm climbing over dozens of railway tracks here, and it's really depressing me to see all these possible impossible departures. Go ahead, sigh, but keep me company a little while longer. Please.

What about your famous GPS?

As lost as I am.

Well . . . well, if what you've just told us is true, then you have to find him again. There's no other answer.

Easy to say . . .

The first waiter—the one who called him Romeo—he must know him.

No. I asked him, but he doesn't know either and hasn't seen him since.

Crap. Then you have to take a compass, and enlarge the circle around where you met, and go to every restaurant inside the circle.

All of them??

Do you have a better idea? You want to unfurl a giant composite sketch of him on the Arc de Triomphe?

But it'll take forever!

Probably, but you've got no choice.

Why?

Why? Because we're getting tired of this! We're sick of listening to you soliloquize in the dark! We don't care about the state of your soul! We don't care! Everyone's had enough, you know. Everyone! What we want is a story. That's why we're here, after all.

Pfff.

Pfff? What's that supposed to mean? Why are you frowning?

I'm afraid of suffering more.

But Mathilde . . . it's wonderful to suffer when you're healthy. It's a privilege! Only dead people don't suffer! Be happy, gorgeous! Go, run, fly, hope, stand still, but *live*! Live a little! Move your well-polished derriere and your musky tutti-frutti legs a little for us, just to see what it's like. Because, beneath all your high-and-mighty talk you moralize just as much as the rest of us, I promise you. So take your medicine, little outraged girl from the nice part of town. Follow through with your beliefs for once. Leave your computer, your comfort zone, your wicked sisters who you talk so negatively about but under whose guardianship you're so happy to stay a little girl; yes, let go of the badmouthing and your stupid cynicism and let go of your mother, who's never coming back, and . . . hey! Where are you going?

I don't believe it . . . my bike! It's my bike! My precious Jeannot! Oh, thank goodness! It's still there! Oh, you're still there, my love. Oh, thank you. Bravo! Well played. Now, let's hurry and get back, because we've got to get our strength back.

I've got a job for you, old girl.

5.

See, Mathilde . . . if you really care about something in life, do whatever it takes not to lose it.

Don't worry, Saint Jean-Baptiste. You couldn't see it under my dress, but I had a pretty nice chain, too.

ACT FOUR

1.

T he sun tickled the carved statues on the building across the street, the citrus juicer grumbled, the kettle sang, the oven clock read 7:42 A.M., and Michel Delpech (or Fugain) (or Polnareff) (or Berger) (or Jonasz) (or Sardou) (or take your pick) bleated good morning.

Julie was checking the expiration date on an organic fairtrade prune soy-milk yogurt. Pauline asked anxiously, "Have you seen Mathilde?"

"No, she'd already gone out when I woke up."

"Again? What is she up to so early?"

"July second . . . we'd better hurry."

"What?"

"The yogurts. Want one?"

"No thanks."

"Look, a lot of this stuff is going bad. It's because of her, too! She never eats anymore!"

"But why is she getting up so early these days? Did she get a job?"

"I have no idea."

"And have you seen the maps in her room? With thumbtacks stuck in them all over the place?"

"Yeah."

"So what is she doing?"

"No idea."

"Does she want to move out?"

Julie ignored this, while Daniel Guichard repeated over and

over again: *le gitan le gitan le gitan le gitan le gitan le gitan le gitan le gitan le gitan le gitan le gitan le gitan le gi . . .*

Help.

2.

M athilde had counted two hundred and twenty-eight restaurants and bars within a fifteen-minute radius around the café where they had met (she figured he might need to get some air or stretch his legs between two dinner services).

She'd already crossed pizzerias, crêperies, tea shops, and Middle Eastern places off her list, along with Indian, Afghan, Tibetan, macrobiotic, and vegetarian restaurants. That kind of cooking didn't require such big knives, she'd decided.

228.

Two hundred and twenty-eight.

One hundred + one hundred + twenty + eight.

A little bit of organization was required: she had photocopied and enlarged the edges of the 28th, 26th, and 22nd arrondissements and taped them up above her dresser before covering them with little red thumbtacks so she could survey them judiciously. (Napoleon himself couldn't have done better.)

She'd started by making phone calls, but she'd quickly realized that it wasn't going to be that easy. She didn't know his last name, was incapable of describing him or saying how old he was, and couldn't specify how long he'd worked there, much less her reasons for looking for him—no, it wasn't for a restaurant inspection, and she didn't want to reserve a table—and so she ended up with nasal-voiced answering machines, harried maître d's, and managers busy tallying up, all of whom eventually told her in their own way to go to hell.

It felt like his retreat from Russia, even before she'd hit the avenues de Wagram or d'Iéna.

What she needed to do was go on the offensive.
Attack. March. March on him.
Show herself to him, smile, joke around, act like an old friend just passing through, or a little sister from the country dumped in Sept-Cinq, or Little Bo Peep who'd lost her sheep, or just some skank (who'd disappear depending on who she met up with).
And she needed to get up early.

Because you could never get anything out of the dining room. Maître d's, café waiters, guys who were tired before they'd even put their vests on, headwaiters who thought they were hot stuff with their blowouts, all those people who changed completely depending on whether they were on duty or not. Who were friendly once they'd put on their uniform and were fishing for tips, but would give you the finger when they were still in street clothes, vacuuming.

What she needed to do was get up early and find the back door. The artists' entrance, the delivery entrance. The badly-lit one that didn't look like anything, that was wedged open with a crate or an empty jar or an oilcan; the one that was half-open now, with Pakistanis, Sri Lankans, Congolese, Filipinos, Ivorians, and other citizens of the United Colors of A Shitty Life coming out and spraying soapy water, and where, from time to time, you could also see zombies with rounder cheeks and lighter skin.

The zombies were rubbing their faces and had enough money to buy pre-rolled cigarettes, and they smoked alone or in groups, one foot braced against the wall, growing more and more silent as the day went on.

Fresh as daisies at the eight o'clock break, calmer at ten,

fried at three, and—paradoxically—completely refreshed at closing time, when they got all chatty again.

Instead of finally going home they talked and laughed, and went over the service, making wisecracks to open the valves and give the stress of the evening time to dissipate in the night air.

In just a few days of this . . . quest, it was, rather than a conquest, so far (she didn't even try to be noticed anymore), Mathilde had learned all of that.

A whole world.

She'd also realized that only having a first name to go on wasn't going to get her very far; that most of these guys only went by their last names, and every time she asked for a Jean-Baptiste she was looked at regretfully, as if she were trying to get her security blanket back from the strict man who'd just closed the school gates. *Jean-Ba*, at a pinch, but *Jean-Baptiste*, no. It was too long.

When she ran into a dishwasher and sensed that her English, or Bengali, or Senegalese, or Tamil, or she didn't even know what, wouldn't be up to the level of his, she gestured at the kitchens and then showed her left hand, folding under the first two joints of a randomly-chosen finger (she couldn't remember exactly which one he was missing); mimed having a big belly with her other hand, and sometimes even a cowlick on top of her head, too.

They—the rare ones who didn't assume she was completely insane—shook their heads and spread their hands.

Then she would hear them whispering among themselves as she walked away:

"Avaluku ina thevai pattudhu?" (What did she want?)

"Nan . . . seriya kandupikikalai aval Spiderman *parkirala aladhu* Elvis Presley *parkirala endru . . ."* (Uh, I couldn't quite tell whether she was looking for Spiderman or Elvis Presley . . .)

"Aanal ninga ina pesuringal? Ina solringa, ungaluku ounum puriyaliya! Ungal Amma Alliance Française Pondicherryla velai saidargal enru ninaithen!" (What are you talking about? You didn't understand any of it, did you! I thought your mother used to work at the Alliance Française in Pondicherry!)

"Nan apojudhu . . . orou china kujandai . . . " (Well, yeah, but I was really little at the time . . .)

Once or twice someone had pointed out a Jean-Baptiste to her who turned out not to be *her* Jean-Baptiste, and on another morning someone showed her a hand missing some fingers— but that wasn't his, either.

News traveled fast on Radio Casserole, and after a week and a half or so it wasn't uncommon for her to be greeted with: "Don't say anything. You're the one looking for an armless cook, right? Heh heh! Nope, he isn't here."

She had become a kind of attraction. The morning's KitKat break. The crazy girl on the bike who crossed things out in her notebook and either bummed a cigarette off you or offered you one.

At the end of the day, she was having fun. She really liked these young people who were always hurrying and not really chatty, but gallant. Always gallant. The youngest ones fascinated her the most. Were they aware of the enormous gulf that stood between them and their civilian friends at this particular time in their lives?

* * *

She set her alarm clock for five A.M., showered at the lowest water pressure so she wouldn't wake up the girls, stuffed her maps into her bag, and went out into Paris at dawn, in the full glory of midsummer.

The rosy, drowsy Paris of deliverymen, market porters, and artisan bakers. She rediscovered views, boulevards, and avenues that she had frequented before, at the same time of the morning, but then she had been exhausted and on automatic pilot, weaving and limping, leaning on—or barely managing to grab—the handlebars of her bike, which served at those times as a balancing weight.

She admired the misty stretches, the rough languor, the half-closed yet already seductive indolence of a city that her poor little eyes, clouded by fatigue, alcohol, and the myxomatosis common to all nameless depressives, hadn't truly seen in a long time, and that remained, whatever was said, whatever was done, *beautiful*.

It was all so picturesque . . . she felt like a tourist, a wanderer, on a sightseeing trip to her own life. She rode very fast, played with bus drivers, slalomed between ungainly rental bikes, followed in Baron Haussmann's tracks, left the working-class atmosphere (what remained of it) of the Place de Clichy far behind her, passed more and more luxurious buildings, recognized the lovely rotunda in the Parc Monceau, asking herself each morning who lived in these over-the-top private mansions, and if these demigods knew how lucky they were; had her breakfast in different local watering holes, watching the prices skyrocket as the arrondissement numbers got lower; people-watched, flipped through *Le Parisien*, turned her back to the television screens, listened to discussions at the bar, got acquainted with boastful, vain, ringing and/or bellowing discussions of horse races and football leagues; got involved when she wanted to, and pedaled fast to make up for the lost time.

She got goose bumps on downslopes and surges of determination going up hills.

Believed.

Fervently.

She improvised a destiny for herself, played with her solitude, made herself into a movie, pretended she was the Mathilde from *Un long dimanche de fiançailles*, searched for a guy who wasn't handsome at all but who wanted to fix her; he had murmured it in her ear one night in the past, and even if she didn't find him, even if this whole thing was just one more rip-off from the Land of Nod, it didn't matter much; it wouldn't matter that much because he had already given her the magnificent gift of awareness that she was on her feet, resolute, an early riser, and *alive*, and that . . . that, in itself, was a lot.

For as long as this handful of cool early mornings lasted, the world . . . at least . . . the world belonged to her.

3.

Belonged?
To other people!
For almost three weeks now she had been searching, getting up at dawn while continuing to work, going to bed with the chickens, eating like a bird and falling asleep disappointed. It was wearing her down.

Mathilde sighed.
But what had she expected?
And the hell was goddamned Cupid up to now?
Well, fatso?
What was this crap?

All the places she had believed in and been inspired by, all the advice and recommendations, all the smoke signals sent from one service door to the next, all the *"Good luck!"*s and *"You say there were rings on the blade? That's Japanese. If I were you I'd start with the Japanese restaurants . . . "*, all the good leads and false hopes, all the meager descriptions and huge questions ("Excuse me, sir, I'm looking for a chef, but . . . uh, I don't know what he goes by, but he's a bit . . . uh . . . pudgy . . . does that tell you anything?"), all the wide eyes and regretful headshakes, the spread hands, the polite sending of her back behind the ropes where they shooed the riffraff, this whole upside-down life, these early mornings and continual disappointments . . . all of it, all, all of it was in vain.

Mathilde was faltering.

Where the hell was he? Did he really work in this neighborhood? Maybe he was an amateur chef, or worked in a school cafeteria or a company restaurant? Or was he just a bullshitter with a bunch of knives? Or a gentle dreamer with no follow-through of his ideas?

And why hadn't he ever called her back? Because he was disappointed? Annoyed? Bitter? Amnesiac?

Because he didn't know how to read?

Because she wasn't his type, or he thought she was still hung up on the shitty poet?

Mathilde wavered.

Did he even exist? Had he *ever* existed?

Maybe she had dreamed it all up. Maybe the letter had been out of its envelope for years. Maybe somebody else had read it way before this. Maybe . . .

Maybe she'd been fucked over by words . . . again.

Speaking of words . . . it was on this street, years ago—she'd forgotten, but it came back to her just then, that her budding writer had turned pale one winter evening.

Pale and deeply emotional because he had seen, in the distance, the silhouette of an old man rushing through the revolving door of the hotel across the street. He had gone white, clutched her arm, and been silent for a long moment before repeating, several times and in every possible ecstatic tone: "Bernard Frank? Was that Bernard Frank? Oh my God . . . Bernard Frank! Don't you get it? It was Bernard Frank!"

No, she didn't get it; she was cold and she wanted to get the metro, but to seem as moved as he was she had said:

"Do you want to go in there? Say hello to him?"

"I couldn't. Besides, that's a luxury hotel. I couldn't even buy you an olive."

And for the whole trip home he had gone on and on about how brilliant and cultured the man was, the amazing books he had written, his style, his coolness, his elegance, blah blah blah. Excitement, mumbo jumbo, yip-yapping, and excessive verbiage of the noble savage, Act II, Scene 3.

She'd listened to him babble with one distracted ear, counting the number of stations left before they got home, and at some point he had added that the man in the white scarf had been best friends with Françoise Sagan, that they had been young, rich, and beautiful together; that they had read and written and danced and gambled and partied together . . . thinking about that had put him into a dreamy state, she remembered.

In a tunnel under the earth on an icy November evening, she had pressed her nose to the window so she wouldn't have to look at his glassy-eyed reflection and had thought about what it must have been like to party with Sagan . . .

That had spoken to her, yes, and now she regretted not having been daring enough to follow him into his luxurious cocoon. Friend of the Gatsbys . . .

Hand in hand, silently, they had dwelt on their doubts and their dreams and their regrets in the bowels of line 9.

And Bernard Frank had died the next day.

Hello, heartache.

Mathilde hit the brakes.

The luxury hotels. She'd forgotten the luxury hotels.

She got off her bike, watching the ballet of concierges swarming around sublime luxury cars in fiscal paradises. Leaning on her handlebars, dumbfounded, she recognized once more the cleverness and all-powerfulness of life.

Because he was there.

Of course he was there.

Behind that grand cut-stone façade, in that exorbitantly-priced hotel on the Rue du Faubourg Saint Honoré, maker of miracles and patron saint of gourmands.

He was there, and words, she had to admit, had called the shots again. They had introduced her to him, and they had sown discord between them, and now they would reunite them.

It was true. Literature tore things apart, and she wasn't always right.

She recognized her faults with relief, and the destructive love of her youth exonerated her at last: it didn't matter if he had used them with more tenderness than he had loved her. He had kept his promise.

* * *

It was almost seven o'clock. A bad time for kitchen reunions.

She'd come back.

She moved away, comforted, and, leaning on old Jeannot, admired her smile in every window on the street, all the way to the corner of the Rue Royale.

Of course it was overpriced, and not always in the best taste, and sometimes hard to carry, but so what. She thought it was beautiful.

4.

Too beautiful, even.

Much too beautiful to be true.

Did you believe that? Are you kidding? What were you hoping for? That she would show up the next morning with a bounce in her step and ask someone to call him, and that he— ta-da!—would appear in a shimmering halo before running toward her in slow motion, with pigeons taking flight and the camera circling around them?

Come on, you bunch of sentimental fools. That only happens in the movies, or the kind of books her ex hated. This is real life, unfortunately, and our dreamer of a heroine got shortchanged: entrance was prohibited, the doors were closed, and the only cameras were surveillance ones.

Okay. This story was beginning to be ridiculous. None of it was funny at all anymore, and Mathilde Salmon (spread the word) was sick and tired of running after a boy.

The character studies took two minutes.

She sat down on the hood of a car, changed her shoes, took out her makeup kit, tied back her hair, powdered her cheeks, lengthened her eyelashes, lined her lips, dabbed perfume on the back of her neck, and stuffed her jacket into her bike's luggage rack before heading back up the street, swaying her hips.

Beautiful, sexy, in a hurry, and dripping with money as she

was, she ignored concierges, bellboys, receptionists, luggage porters, maids, and clients.

Step aside.

Step aside, little people; you only get in the way.

Walking on a carpet as thick as her nerve, she went down hallways, ignored the questions and other remarks in Russian and English that people addressed to her along the way; arranged an invisible stole around her shoulders, searched for the dining room, dodged a vacuum cleaner, smiled in apology, spied the kitchens, pushed the door open, and collared the first person she saw:

"I need to see Jean-Baptiste immediately. Call him for me, please."

5.

"Who? Vincent?"

"No (disdainfully), Jean-Baptiste. I just told you. The one who uses Japanese knives."

"Ohh, right, Jibé (scornfully). He doesn't work here anymore."

And all of a sudden Mathilde wasn't beautiful anymore. Or rich, or sexy, or proud. Or anything at all.

She closed her eyes and waited for someone to throw her out. A big, tough-looking guy was already coming toward her, wiping his hands.

"Miss? Are you lost?"

She said yes, and he showed her the exit.

But there must have been something in the sadness of her expression that told him she was truly crushed, and ugly, and miserable, because he added:

"Do you know him? Be careful . . . I thought I knew him too, and then . . . I got taken for a ride anyway. It was a while ago, though. I told him, by the way, I told him . . . but I don't know what's gotten into him, because he's not very accommodating, is he? Nope, not accommodating at all. He didn't show up to work for weeks. He fed me line after line of bullshit, and then he left."

"Do you know where I can find him?"

"No, I have no idea. And I don't want to know, to tell you the truth. He really left us in the shit, too, in the middle of high season like that. Oh yeah, I remember . . . one morning he showed up and he just wasn't the same anymore. Nothing interested him. He couldn't tell the difference between a watermelon and a whelk anymore, the pigheaded fool. First he had to take some time off work because he burned himself, and then it happened again and we had to send him to the emergency room, and when he came back he wasn't even the same person. He couldn't concentrate. 'I just don't like it anymore,' was all he could tell me. He emptied out his locker and settled his accounts and left, and you can go out the same door. And if you ever see him, tell him to give me back my Grimod. He'll know what it means."

Making her way back past the kitchen staff, Mathilde sensed that she was disturbing them, that she should hurry up. Access here, she remembered, was forbidden to salespeople and vendors and people looking for other people and all other intruders foreign to the world of the hash slingers.

Ousted.

She was walking toward her beautiful Aston Martin with the broken dynamo when the first guy she had spoken to touched her elbow.

"Is it you?"

"Excuse me?"

"Are you the girl from the Arc de Triomphe?"

It hurt when she smiled and she realized she had bitten her lip until it bled.

"I wasn't sure. He's in the country. He went back to work for his uncle. In Périgueux."

Sweet Jesus. Périgueux. It might as well be Australia.

"Does he have a phone number?"

"I don't know it. Do you have something to write with? I'll

give you the name of the restaurant. It's not like here, you know. It'll be easier to find him."

She carefully wrote down what he told her, and then looked up to thank him:

"Why are you looking at me like that?" she asked, startled.

"No reason."

He turned around and walked a few steps away before changing his mind. "Hey!"

"Yeah?"

"What was in your bag, exactly?"

"An atlas."

"Oh, really?"

He seemed disappointed.

6.

Mathilde thought about going home to grab her laptop and a toothbru—no. They'd already lost enough time.

She hesitated at the first red light: wait, goddammit, which station for Périgueux? Montparnasse or Austerlitz?

Okay, little emperor, you've been the third wheel since the beginning, so I'll trust you all the way. They say it was your greatest tactical victory, and I'm pretty hopeless when it comes to tactics. So, Austerlitz it is.

Don't let me down, okay?

She chained her bike to a parapet and made a dash for the ticket windows.

"One-way or round-trip?" a friendly clerk in a mauve vest asked her.

Yikes. One-way. It was already complicated enough.

"Just one-way for now, please."

And forward-facing, if possible, for once.

FINAL ACT

1.

I t was a long day of waiting. First in the Gare d'Austerlitz, and then in the station in Limoges, and finally in the streets of old Périgueux.

Even though she'd never been here, this place brought back a lot of memories. D'Artagnan was there, everywhere, dashing into taverns exclaiming: "Greetings, you rogue! Greetings, you devil of a barkeep! Our best wine!" Otherwise there were bottles of walnut oil, preserves, stuffed duck necks, and the same logo-emblazoned clothing as everywhere else in the whole world.

The fleur-de-lis had had a setback in the place. In China, it must be said, they embroidered them a lot more cheaply.

Ah well . . . it was our world, and you had to love it. These old stones, which told swashbuckling historical romances . . . they didn't hurt, either.

Mathilde wandered around, killing time, because she had decided to wait for the end of the dinner service. To reveal herself to him in the twilight. Not because it was more romantic, but because she was terrified.

She may have acted like an idle onlooker observing the local lifestyle, but the simple truth is that our young friend was scared. The anger of the head chef who had sent her away had rattled her. Maybe the guy in question really was crazy. Maybe she was walking into a lion's den . . . or worse, into the clutches of a half-wit. Or someone who really didn't give a shit about the poor little rich girl from the Champs-Élysées with her false promises and her words, who remembered . . .

Or, much, much worse even than that, someone who would say to her in a few hours, pointing to the clock:
"Sorry. We're not serving anymore."

Yeah, it was entirely possible that she was about to lose another life to this idiotic game she had invented to pass the time.
God help me.
Greetings, barkeep! An ice-cold Coke to help the little girl pluck up some courage!

At the Place du Marché she stood on her tiptoes to photograph a pretty statue of a pilgrim on the Route of Santiago de Compostela.
Click. Holiday memory.
Worst-case scenario, if things really went badly, she'd make it her desktop background.
Like a Post-it stuck up to remind her forever how risky it was to love your neighbor, and to believe again.

Quarter to midnight. She'd spent two hours loitering on a low wall across from Unky's Inn.

The place was stylish, full of wooden beams and copper pots and laughter and the tinkling of silverware and glasses. D'Artagnan and his gang would have loved it.

The last slowpokes were finally rousing themselves enough to pay their checks, and the Coke wasn't having any effect anymore. Mathilde rubbed her stomach, begging it to behave itself for just a little while longer.

Her palms were sticky with perspiration.

* * *

Now the customers were all gone, but there were still people moving around the room. A lady brought the blackboard in from outside the front door. A young man, motorcycle helmet under one arm, said goodbye to her before lighting a cigarette and taking off; another put new place settings on tables that had just been vacated, while a big man with a mustache in a vintner's apron (the uncle?) was busy behind a counter.

Then, nothing more.

Mathilde was seething.

Swear words bubbled up inside her and forced their way out between her teeth, clenched as they were.

A murmuring in the night:

"Fuck, what the hell are they doing in there, goddammit? Come on, come on, get lost, assholes. Get lost. And you; when the hell will you be coming out? Haven't you driven me crazy enough yet? Come on, for God's sake, put the stuffed duck necks down and come out of that greasy spoon . . . "

Ten minutes later, the lady and the young table-setter finally reappeared and kissed each other on the cheek directly in front of her before going off in opposite directions. All the lights in the restaurant went out.

"Hey!" she exclaimed, jumping up and crossing the street at a run. "I'm not going to sleep out here!"

She bumped into tables, knocked over a chair, swore under her breath, and, like a moth, headed toward the only source of light left to guide her, shining through the porthole of a kitchen door.

She pushed it open slowly, holding her breath, steeling her dignity, her nerves, and her gut.

A man in a white jacket was concentrating on his hands.

He was standing, busily fiddling with something in front of him on a stainless-steel work surface.

"You can go, I'll lock up. But leave me your keys; I forgot mine again," he said, not taking his eyes off his work.

She started.

She recognized his voice, low as it was.

"By the way, did you let Pierrot know about the veal sweet-breads?"

And because, alas, no, she hadn't let Pierrot know, he finally looked up.

3.

His face manifested neither surprise, nor happiness, nor astonishment.

Zilch.

He looked at her.

He looked at her for . . . hard to say how long. Seconds aren't really seconds at times like this; they're rare and count triple. For an eternity, let's say.

And she . . . she was speechless. First she was drained, and then it was okay. Her part of the work was done.

She didn't move a muscle. It was his turn now. His turn to take over their story. To say something stupid and jeopardize everything, or to say . . . she didn't know, something that would finally let her sit down and breathe.

He had sensed all of that. He was struggling for words; it showed in his face. Words, fatigue, and his memories. That he was groping. That he was on the point of . . . and then biting it back. That he was scared, and that he was as deeply enmeshed in this as she was.

He looked down again, and went back to what had been absorbing his attention. To buy some time, and because he was smarter when his hands were occupied.

A long, rectangular blue stone was on the counter in front of him. He was sharpening his knives.

She watched him.

*

They played Mikado with their nerves, and the calm, regular scraping sound soothed them both. These, they might both have been telling themselves, were so many minutes bought before everything might crumble.

He inspected the blade, testing its sharpness by letting it slide in a curve over his left thumbnail, then turned it around and went back to work.

A sort of dark paste had formed on the stone. He traced loops in it, and figure eights, and whorls, bearing down with all his weight on the three fingers guiding the steel.

Fascinated, she studied the short fingernails whitening with effort, the hardened and cut pads of flesh at their tips, and, hidden beneath the ebony sleeve, the famous abbreviated ring finger.

That finger, crippled, soft, and pale . . . she wanted to touch it.

Without sparing her a glance, he pulled a bowl of water toward him and moistened the stone with gentle strokes of his hand.

The scraping of the blade, the stormy little flutterings of their hearts, which had been pent up for too long, the humming of the walk-in freezer in the distance, cradled them for another moment, and then there were footsteps in the next room, the CLACK! of a circuit breaker, the noise of a door closing and a pair of shutters being drawn, and then one—no, two—locks clicking.

They found themselves plunged into darkness, and it was only then that she saw him smile. She could hear his dimples in his voice.

"Too bad. Like I just told you, I forgot my keys."

He was already savoring this. She still hadn't spoken. She groped behind her and found a stool, pulled it over and sat down across from him.

After all the noise, silence again.

"I'm happy," he murmured.
She had reopened the little cut on her lower lip. Was it his turn to talk? Oh dear, no, not now. She was too tired. She'd come to him because he hadn't stolen from her; please, let him keep up that momentum.
She played with her wounded lip, to gain a few more seconds.
She bit it where it hurt the most, and sucked away her own blood.
"You've lost weight," he said.
"You too."
"Yeah . . . me too. More than you. But I had more to lose, right?"
She smiled in the dark.
He rocked back and forth, as if he wanted to make a hollow in the stone.

After another minute, or two, or three, or maybe a thousand, he added, his voice still low:
"I thought that you . . . that I . . . no . . . nothing."
Sccccritch! A fly electrocuted itself in the bluish halo of a trap set near the corridor.

"Are you hungry?" he asked after a time, looking at her as if he'd never seen her before in his life.
"Yes."
"Me too."
She smiled, and it hurt, and she licked her lips, because it hurt.
She salivated on her lip a little, to cauterize it, and he carefully wiped his big knife.

"Take your clothes off."

YANN

One, the Ball

I'm closing this week. I approve the final orders, turn off the machines, and make sure the drawers and all the display cases are locked.

I'll admit that this is what bores me the most. I feel like a little country jeweler carefully locking up his gold-plated necklaces and bracelets every night, but Eric, my colleague in the 5th Arrondissement, all but got caught stealing more than 3,000 bucks worth of hardware last month, and I know he's not out of the woods with that whole thing.

Oh, no one has said he's a thief; it's just understood, that's all.

"You know, sometimes I think it's the best thing that could have happened to me. Having to give them my badge and mollify my girlfriend's thwarted dreams of store credit. Not taking the commuter train anymore; not starting the day with that humiliation. Barely awake and already cooped up, packed in like sardines, a slave to the grind. All these suburbanites, haggard and resigned just like you, reading the same bullshit stories as you in the same free newspapers at exactly the same time as you. I swear, that's what depresses me the most," he had confided to me, sighing, while we took part in a training day on their new sales software. "Yeah . . . too bad I still love my girlfriend . . . "

We had exchanged a smile and then a new speaker came on, and we shut up.

(If you got in that lady's bad books she'd tell our boss, and we'd lose our *Business, Care & Involvement* bonus.)

(The brownnoser.)

So anyway, I lock everything up.

Then I turn off the showroom lights and take the freight elevator and walk kilometers of hallways lit only by emergency lights.

I hurry, because of the alarm.

I look for my locker in the changing room and punch in a code—another one, the tenth of the day, I'm pretty sure—and change my vest ("Yann, how can I help you?") for a shabby old peacoat that makes it clear to the whole world that poor little Yann can no longer do anything for anyone. I hurry, again, because of *another* alarm, and end up in a blind alley behind the Boulevard Haussmann between two rows of garbage cans and a dog breeder making the rounds.

When he has the big Doberman we smoke a cigarette while chatting about the weather and custom cars and double-clutch transmissions (well, he chats and I try to come up with appropriate responses), and when it's the other one, the Rottweiler, I wait until I'm at the end of the cul-de-sac before I relax.

It's not the dog's teeth that scare me; it's the way he looks at me.

I always wondered who reads *Détective* magazine. The answer is, this guy does.

This guy . . . a headline like "Lili, age three, beaten to death, raped, tortured, and burned alive" . . . that turns him on, as they say. It turns him on a lot.

Tonight I'm the one who pulled out my cigarette pack first. He's anxious because one of his dog's puppies—not this one, another one, one that only does parking—has a testicle that isn't dropping.

I was about to say how nice that was, and stopped myself just in time.

It wasn't funny at all. It was tragic, even. No ball, no pedigree, and no pedigree, no money.

"It'll drop eventually, right?"

He didn't seem too convinced. "Well . . . maybe. Maybe yes, maybe no. *Insha'Allah* . . . heaven knows."

Poor Allah, I thought, walking away. I hope He has someone in the prayer office who sorts through these things before putting them in the pipeline.

Two, Demons

The clock on the American pharmacy informs me that it's already 10:10 P.M. and that the temperature is -5°.

There's no one expecting me. Mélanie's still stuck at one of her seminars and it's too late to go to a movie.

I head for the nearest metro station, and then change my mind. I can't go to a club now; I'll keel over.

I need to walk. I need to go home on foot, and cross Paris, slapping my demons away with my hands and swatting them with my hat.

I need to suffer, to be cold, to be hungry, and to take advantage of finally being alone to collapse into bed, dead tired.

I've been sleeping badly for months. I don't like my school, I don't like my schedule, I don't like my professors or the smell of the locker rooms or the cafeteria or the idiots surrounding me. At age twenty-six I have the same insomnia I had at age twelve, except that at age twenty-six it's a thousand times worse, because I got myself into this mess all alone. Me. I can't blame my parents, and I don't even have vacations anymore . . .

What have I done?

What?

What have you done?

It's true! But what have you done now, moron?

I curse myself out loud the whole way home, because the lukewarm breath of my anger keeps the tip of my nose warm.

Most of the bums are in hidey-holes somewhere; the ones who are drinking to get through the night will be dead by morning; the Seine is ink-black, slow and sluggish. Winding between the piles of the Pont-Neuf it creates a noiseless indraught. It's on the hunt, stalking the weary, the exhausted employees, the talentless little dreamers and the people who question themselves in the night. It picks out the ones without confidence and the slippery parapets. *Come on*, it murmurs. *Come on, it's only me . . . go ahead . . . we've known each other for so long . . .*

I imagine its icy touch, the clothing billowing out before weighing you down, the shock, the cry torn out of you, the panic. Everyone imagines that, don't they?

Yes. Of course they do. Anyone who passes a river as part of their daily routine has that kind of vertigo.

It's comforting.

Diversion:

Text from Mélanie: "Wiped out going to bed shit weather xx," with a little "kiss" doodad at the end. (Some winking yellow thing with big lips.) (Emoticons, that's what they're called.)

Emoticon. The name is as vulgar as the thing. I hate that lazy crap. Instead of expressing a feeling, you take a shortcut. You press a button and all the smiles in the world are exactly the same. The joys, doubts, sorrow, anger; everything has the same face. All the desires of the heart, reduced to five hideous little circles.

Goddamn. What "progress."

"Goodnight," I answer. "All my love."

That's much better isn't it?

No. Not much. Still, it's a kiss in three words, though. And the apostrophe looks nice . . .

There aren't many guys left who take the trouble to text apostrophes these days. Are they the same ones who imagine what it's like to drown?

I'm afraid the answer might actually be yes.

Good God, I'm a sad sack tonight.

Sorry.

It's been that way for a while. The discouragement, the lyrical/loserish flights of fancy, the need to confront other people—all other people—to muddy the waters. Mélanie thinks it's because of the weather (late winter, lack of sunlight, seasonal depression) and professional stagnation (no sign of the promises that were made to me, lack of ambition, disillusionment). Okay. Why not?

She's lucky; she belongs to that category of human beings who find causes and solutions for everything: dust mites, the right to vote for immigrants, the closure of the drugstore on the Rue Daguerre, her dad's warts, and my depression. I envy her, in a way. I'd like to be like that.

I'd love for everything to be that simple in my head, that easy, that . . . *materializable.*

Never to have doubts. Always to find suspects, culprits, guilty parties. To rush in, take drastic action, command, judge, hack away, sacrifice, and have the certainty that my la-di-da existentialist vapors will vanish when spring comes, and disappear completely with 200 more euros on my paycheck . . .

Unfortunately, though, I don't believe that for one second.

I'll be twenty-seven in June, and I can't decide if that's still young or if I'm old already. I can't tell which side of the border I belong on. It's very fuzzy, this whole thing. From a distance people think I'm a teenager, and close-up I look like an old fart. An old fart disguised as a high-school student: the same fake cheerfulness, the same Converses, the same jeans, the same haircut, and the same Chuck Palahniuk novels in the same battered backpack.

A schizo. A stowaway. An early-21st-century young man, born in a wealthy country and raised by loving parents, a little boy who had everything: kisses, hugs, birthday parties, video-game systems, plenty of familiarity with the multimedia library, visits from the tooth fairy, Harry Potter books, Pokémon and Yu-Gi-Oh and Magic cards, hamsters, replacement hamsters, unlimited packages, trips to England, trendy sweats, and all the rest, but not only that.

Not only that.

A little boy born at the very end of the 20th century, who has been told since he was old enough to throw his own candy wrappers in the wastebasket that nature is suffering because of him, that the forests are disappearing for the sake of the palm oil in his *pains au chocolat,* that the ice caps melt a little more whenever Mommy starts her car engine, that all the wild animals are dying out, and that if he doesn't turn the faucet off every time he brushes his teeth, well, all of this will be partly his fault.

Next, an inquisitive and well-behaved student who, his history books tell him, should be ashamed of having been born white, greedy, lazy, a colonizer, an informer, and an accomplice, while the geography texts harangue him year after year with alarming figures of global overpopulation, industrialization, desertification, shortages of air and water and fossil fuel and arable land. Not to mention the French books, which always end up making you hate reading by forcing you to screw everything up—*Identify and arrange in order the lexical field of sensuality in this Baudelaire poem*; boom, end of the line, the whole world loses its hard-on—with language, reminding you every year how much you were a Shit with a capital S; and the last year of high school, which is just a concentrated recap of all the other stuff, only even more implacable: *Okay, you little floppy-dicked white nonentity, whose stupid accent is a joke to the rest of the world, identify and arrange in order the lexical field of the wastefulness of your civilization, please. You have four hours.*

(Hey, hey! Rough copy in the yellow wastebasket, please.)

And when this anxiety-producing edification is finally ingested, digested, understood, repeated in exam books, and reported in the senior exam pass-rate statistics, before you know it I've added several years of study on top of that so you don't get stuck too fast in the barriers of the future.

And you, you poor schmuck, you do everything by the book: study sessions, exams, degrees, internships.

Unpaid internships, non-remunerated internships, internships without financial compensation, internships for honor and internships for glory. CVs. CVs with a nice photo. CVs on paper and online and 3-D and video, whatever you want, voilà, anything. Cover letters. Cover e-mails. Cover videos. All that mumbo jumbo and hot air, where you don't even know what to make up anymore because you've already stopped believing in it, you're already so depressed by it, by fighting so hard, so early on, just to have the right to pay your dues like everyone else.

But you keep going. You keep on, valiantly: career offices, job centers, job fairs, headhunters, classified ads, job alerts, recruitment platforms, codes to access your candidate space, subscriptions to job boards, false hopes, interviews lost in advance, Facebook-makers who won't even assess you in your dreams, your godfather's brother-in-law who's going to talk to his friends in the Lions Club, the crazy ex-girlfriend, you know I still kind of want to tell you to go fuck yourself, but doesn't your dad own a factory? Temporary agencies, inevitable string-pulling, half-assed string-pulling, crooked string-pulling, job sites that become more and more expensive to access and HR assistants who become less and less gracious . . . yeah, you've always insisted, you've never littered in your whole life, or put

your feet up on the metro seat across from you, even when it
was really late at night, even when you were completely fried;
even when you were the only one in the whole train car, and
you got your degree without causing any trouble to anyone,
but . . . nope. No luck. There are no jobs. No work for you.

No, there's nothing. You can't mean that; are you sure? I
can't believe that. You could still talk to your neighbor, the one
that lives on your left . . .

Hey! Boyo! Wake up! We're in an economic crisis! Listen
to the news instead of learning a profession; it'll be less a waste
of your time. What's that? You don't understand? Listen
closely, sweetie, and don't move, because I'm going to sum up
the situation for you:

You're young, you're European, and you're a nice guy?
You're in for a hell of a rough time, my friend.

People carp at you endlessly about your country's national
debt reaching a hundred thousand billion zillion dollars; your
money will soon be worthless, and if you don't speak Chinese it's
not even worth trying; Qatar is in the process of buying us all;
Europe is finished, the West is kaput, and the planet is fucked.

That's all.

Bread and circuses. This is it. We're there.

Believe you me, little boy, there's nothing left to do but
watch football while we wait for the apocalypse.

Go ahead. Have a lie-down. *Fly Emirates* and shut up.

And stop flailing around like that. Stop clicking and making phone calls and running around applying for jobs everywhere, please. It's bad for the ozone layer.

* * *

I can't feel my feet anymore. At the top of the Boulevard

Saint-Michel, just after the Luxembourg Gardens greenhouses, a pair of cops are stopping distracted, exhausted drivers.

As I pass them, head down and nose buried in my scarf, I hear them asking for the ID papers of a young woman in a blue down jacket. I don't know if it's because of the cold or the number of points on her driver's license, but she looks petrified. She rummages nervously in her bag for her papers and drops a bunch of keys on the ground. There's a baby sleeping in a car seat. She shouldn't drive so fast, because her car is an ancient Mini. The old model, the one designed by Sir Alec Issigonis. That pure marvel.

"No, but it's so the heater will run," I hear her say.

"Please," the junior officer says. "Turn off the engine right now. This won't take long."

I go on my way, mystified.

What has this country become?

This democratic hole, where the forces of law and order have nothing better to do than set endless traps for its most harmless citizens? What does it mean, exactly?

Are the coffers as empty as all that?

And who are these guys, who do this job? Who get paid to go out and harass a woman at midnight on a Tuesday in February because one of her headlights is out or her license plate is a bit loose? What the hell is that? And when they insist that she turn off her engine when it's -6° outside even though there's a little one asleep in the passenger seat; what's going through their heads?

Is it that satisfying, to be a public servant?

And what about you? What the hell is your deal? This outraged little shithead with your endless moralizing speeches, who isn't even capable of coming to the defense of a pretty mother. A girl driving a Mini 1000, even. What kind of crap is that?

Do you also have a ball that hasn't dropped?

Or maybe it froze . . .

Diversion:

By the time he designed the Mini, Issigonis had already delivered the Morris Minor and the Austin 1100.

Not too shabby.

When William Morris, the big boss, saw the Minor for the first time, he was horrified. *Holy God*, he said, *a poached egg.*

The Minor was a considerable success.

But Issi believed he'd never get his f***ing diploma in mechanical engineering, which he failed three times in a row because of the math part. It was design that saved him. When it came to design he was a prince. The rules and postulates and laws of physics and mathematics bored him to tears; and worse, according to him, they were *the enemy of every truly creative man.* Nor did he give a shit about commercial policies, predictions, business plans, market studies, and all those other precursors of modern marketing. He was a curmudgeon.

He maintained that, to design a new car, the first rule was not to copy the competition. He was independent, free, and obstinate, and didn't have much respect for anything that came out of the intense brainstorming sessions of research departments. It was he who coined the wonderful phrase: *A camel is a horse designed by committee.*

I know all this because I took a university trip (that higher education dear to my heart and to my parents' small economies) (which isn't actually serving any purpose for me at this particular moment in time) to the Design Museum in London.

Wow, what a lovely souvenir . . .

Almost home. It's so cold that the lion in the Place Denfert-

Rochereau seems to have curled up in a little ball on its pedestal like a big, irritated tomcat.

I'd chosen that route because I also drew well and—no offense to Sir Alec—I was good at math. I mean, not good enough to get into the top, top schools, but . . . and I was also curious. Curious about the arts and history and art history, and the decorative arts and technology and the industrial world, and industrial technology and ergonomics and morphology, and things and people and furniture and fashion and textiles and typography and graphic design and . . . well, everything, actually. Everything, all the time, and from every era. The only glitch was that I'm not talented. No, really, I'm not. I've learned that, too. Not talented, and absolutely not wired to have the pride or the genius to create *something else*. The university taught me that, at least—to understand both myself and the distance separating me from a Gio Ponti or a Jonathan Ive, for example. (I know, I know, it's become very uncool to say nice things about the vice president of design at Apple, but being considered uncool because I piously and very humbly admit to the great respect I have for him, well, I'm fine with that.)

I should have gotten a degree in documentary filmmaking and applied for a job at the Bibliothèque des Arts et Métiers or the library at ENSCI instead; I would have been very happy. My only talent is recognizing other people's.

A weakness of mine that was diagnosed during one of my countless job interviews.

"Basically, young man, you're a dilettante."

Shit.
Is that bad?

Clearly, I should have set my sights on a less cruel industry (because in the world of design, you're either a visionary or you're completely worthless) (I would have lost all my illusions in the battle, but not my ideals). Less cruel, and better suited to my dilettantism. But the saddest thing, the biggest shame, is that I was afraid—if I followed my natural inclinations—of not having a job.

Ha ha! That Yann! He modeled his life a little too well . . .
Like a camel, you might say.

Start of the Rue Boulard. I'm warming up. Good thing, because icicles were starting to form on me.

Where was I? Oh yeah. My destiny.

So. So far, and to make a long story short, I have a degree from a design school and I'm . . . uh . . . what would you call it . . . a demonstrator. That's it, a demonstrator of little Korean robots designed for domestic, recreational, and household use by domestic, recreational, and household classes.

The little dachshund vacuum that goes back into its corner all by itself once it's licked up all the dust; the light-up speakers that create different atmospheres depending on what kind of music they're playing; the showerhead that's also an intergalactic digital radio, and the intelligent refrigerator that tells you everything that's inside it whenever it recognizes your voice: how much is left, expiration dates, number of calories in the food, combinations of ingredients, tips on how to use leftovers, blah blah blah.

Isn't that great?

Gio Ponti would be floored.

I have a permanent contract (yes, a permanent contract, the One Ring, the Black Lotus, the Holy Grail) (*Hanenim Kamsa hamnida*) ("Thank you God," in Korean) in a kind of high-tech kiosk that presents these incredible marvels to a flabbergasted Europe.

In other words, I'm a sales representative for Dartyyongg.

But hey, it's only temporary, right?

Yes it is. Yes, it is. Yes it is.

Go to bed, little Miko.

Not only have I not killed the demons, you might say I've gotten them all riled up.

What an idiot.

After punching in the last code of the day, I wedge a piece of cardboard into the gap between the door and the jamb to keep it from closing and locking, and do the same with the hall door.

If only, I sigh, if only the last bum in the neighborhood who hasn't already made tracks at this time of night could have the good taste (and weakness) to come and warm up in my little setup here, it would be good for my ego.

I go up the two flights of stairs at a run so as not to lose a toe, peel a banana and soak it in the last of the vodka, empty the hot water tank, and finally drop.

Three, the Chamonix

Today I finish earlier than usual, but I'm still a bachelor. Mélanie doesn't get back until Thursday.

I just talked to her on the phone: the hotel isn't as nice as she thought it would be, the spa is closed, and her team is useless.

Okay.

(She's a medical rep, and the lab that employs her regularly organizes remotivation seminars to help them overcome the major trauma of generic medications.)

"Are you going to do the shopping?"

Of course. Of course I'm going to do the shopping. I've been stuck doing the shopping for two years, I'm not going to pick tonight to revolutionize our life as a couple.

"And don't forget the loyalty card. The last time, you lost us at least sixty points. I figured it out."

Mélanie is an informed consumer. Sixty points is a lot.

"No, no, I won't forget. Well, I'll let you go, because I have to go get little Woof-Woof out."

"Sorry?"

"My little vacuum cleaner."

"Oh . . . "

When she says "Oh . . . " like that, I wonder what she's really thinking. Is she distressed? Does she talk about me to her colleagues? Does she say to them, "My partner sells Woof-Woofs in various colors"?

I doubt it. She thought she'd met the next Philippe Starck but she's ended up with Overstock.com, I'm afraid. Plus I'm pretty sure she thinks I spend my days playing around with gadgets. If she only knew. It's easier to peddle anticoagulants than it is a Frigidaire that breaks your balls every time you go into the kitchen. Well, whatever. I'm finishing earlier, but I'm not going to rush off to do the shopping at Franprix because I saw that there's a Sidney Lumet festival showing at the Grand Action, and they're playing *Running on Empty* at nine o'clock tonight.

Thank you, life.

I saw that movie with my cousin (probably even in the same theater) when I was fifteen, around the same age as River Phoenix when he played Danny Pope, and it affected me so much that I got run over by a bus as I was leaving the theater. It's true. Four broken toes out of ten.

Let's just say that the prospect of seeing it again made my heart beat faster, because—and this is a secret Mélanie doesn't know—I've been building up loyalty points in my own way, too.

I decide to run by the house to change and eat something before finding a bike share.

(Bikes are nice when you come out after seeing a great movie; the headlight is like a projector, and the most beautiful scenes light your way in the night.)

When I get to my landing, a half-eaten sandwich in one hand and my uninteresting mail in the other, I suddenly find myself nose-to-nose with a huge piece of furniture. A sort of armoire in blue Formica. It's sitting at a diagonal, blocking my way, and since I'm not armless I put my stuff down to shove it over a meter or so. As I'm doing this I hear a sharp little voice:

"Mommy! Mommy! There's a man who's stuck!"

Then a voice of medium pitch:

"Do you hear that, Isaac? Did you hear what your daughter just said? Do something with that thing!"

And finally the deep voice of Papa Bear:

"WOMEN! BLOODY WOMEN! YOU WANT ME TO DIE, IS THAT IT? YOU WANT ME TO BE CRUSHED UNDER THE WEIGHT OF THAT ATROCIOUS THING SO YOU CAN GET MY INHERITANCE? NEVER! NEVER, DO YOU HEAR ME? I'LL NEVER LEAVE YOU GRANDPAPA'S TREASURES!" (Then, in a softer voice for my benefit: "Sorry, neighbor, sorry! Can you get through?")

I look up and see, above the curve of the fourth-floor railing, a ruddy face framed by a bushy beard and, between the bars, two little Goldilocks looking at me gravely.

"No problem," I say.

He gives me a wave and I move away, turning my key as delicately as possible so I can overhear the rest of the scene.

"Come on, girls. You'll catch cold."

But Mama Bear is having none of it:

"What about Hans?"

"Hans is an ass. We had a difference of opinion right away and he dumped me with this piece of crap on the second floor. There you go, if you want to know everything! There's the truth for you! HANS-IS-AN-ASS! (pronouncing each syllable distinctly, and loud enough for the whole building to hear). Come on, girls, come in now, or I'll shut you up in this piece of garbage your mother paid two hundred euros to a bandit for. Vintage, vintage . . . I couldn't care less about vintage. Hurry up, little chickens! Your lord and master is hungry!"

"Oh ho, let's be very clear on that score, my friend: as long as my pretty buffet is in the stairwell, you're not getting any dinner."

"VERY WELL, LITTLE MADAM! VERY WELL! IN THAT CASE, I'M GOING TO EAT YOUR CHILDREN!"

The man roars like an ogre and a bunch of shrill little shrieks echo off the walls of the stairwell.

I turn around in wonderment, dazzled by the glitters of a magic sparkler.

Their door slams and, go figure, I no longer have any desire to go home.

I'll go out for a kebab.

* * *

I head back down the stairs, musing.

I've passed her once or twice in the mornings, taking her daughters to school. She's always disheveled, always in a rush, and always polite. Mélanie grumbles because she parks her stroller just anywhere in the lobby, a stroller full of toys, pails, sand, and crumbs. When there are cases of bottled water or milk at the bottom of the stairs I carry them up and put them down on the first steps leading up from our landing, so it's as if they've made a little more than half the journey all by themselves.

Mélanie rolls her eyes: a deliveryman *and* a demonstrator. It's too much.

One day, when the mother from the fourth floor thanked me too fervently for these modest little bits of help, I made her feel better by telling her that, in recompense, I'd helped myself to a forgotten Chamonix cookie or two from the bottom of the stroller. I heard her laugh from a few floors away, and the next day there was a whole package of them on my doorstep.

I didn't tell Mélanie.

This is the first time I've seen the father's face, but I think I can hear his footsteps sometimes, late at night.

I know he has a subscription to *La Gazette Drouot*, because I see it sticking out of their mailbox, and I also know he drives a Mercedes station wagon, because it has the same newspapers folded up on the dashboard.

One morning I saw him take a parking ticket off his windshield and use it to pick up a pile of dog crap before tossing the whole bundle in the gutter.

That's all I know about them. We haven't lived in the building very long, though.

Grandpapa's treasures. I smiled comfortably.

It was charming, their little scene. They'd shouted at each other like street-theater actors, really. Like something out of an operetta. His voice, booming out rather than yelling: Bloody women! Vintage! Vintage! (pronounced "vaintage") Very well, little madam!—his part of the libretto was still ringing in my ears.

I smiled as I made my way back down the stairs.

I smiled in the darkness because the timer chose that minute to shut off the lights, and because I was happy, there in the dark, replaying that little gift from heaven in my mind: a tiny taste of Parisian life, in the style of Offenbach.

I hadn't even put an eyelash out the front door when an icy gust brought me back to the here and now.

God, I'm slow on the uptake. I turned on my heel and hightailed it back up the stairs.

FOUR, THE MARQUISE

I t *is* in your way, isn't it?"

He wasn't humming anymore. He was almost as wide as his doorway. He wore a plaid vest, a striped shirt, and a dotted bow tie, with all the colors of the rainbow visible in wool, cotton, and silk. I don't know if it was because of his shortness, the colorful brocade vest, or the beard, but he reminded me of the boisterous, larger-than-life character Gareth in *Four Weddings and a Funeral*. His little daughters had already come back out and stared at me with the same anxious faces as before. But it was all an act. I knew these girls had a flair for drama, and that their apparent gravity was all just part of the show. They wanted to keep performing.

"No, no, not at all! I was just wondering if I could help you carry it up to your apartme—"

Without even letting me finish, he turned and thundered:

"Alice! I've finally met your lover! He's a very handsome young man! Well done, my love!"

"Who . . . who are you talking about?" chirped the unfaithful wife.

And Alice came out.
And Alice made her appearance.

I'm not sure which of those two expressions best captures the effect I'm trying to convey. The upstairs neighbor, the *maman* with the stroller, the disseminator of crumbs and cartons of milk, came nearer. She recognized me and smiled. And if, as she smiled at me like that, looking me straight in the eye, she hadn't also leaned against her husband's shoulder (she was much taller than him) and slipped a careless arm around his neck, I would have fallen in love with her right then and there. Now, immediately, and forever. But unfortunately there was that detail—that "careless"—that compromised our chances for bliss. Because that was what made her so beautiful and so sexy. It was that ease, that confidence, that instinctive way she'd leaned against him, even here on their doorstep, with a dish towel in her hand, for no reason at all. Just to ask a question. It was because she adored her little blusterer of a husband (you could feel it), who loved her in return (you could see it), and who must make love to her all the time, that she could allow herself to turn me on that way, with such vulgar guilelessness.

Whoa, whoa, whoa, little mother . . . that was hot.

Of course, at the time, I was too disturbed to analyze everything that was going through my head, and contented myself with repeating my offer to help.

"Oh, thank you! That's so kind," she exclaimed, and then she was taking her husband's jacket off as if it were a satin cape.

Respecting the ceremony, as it were, but shoving him very slightly forward at the same time.

Very Mary Poppins and Rocky Balboa.

He grumbled, undoing his cuff links and handing them to one of his daughters and then removing his bow tie and giving it to the other daughter. Then he pushed up the sleeves of his shirt (it was of very fine cotton and I really wanted to stroke it) and turned to me.

He was perfectly round, like a fireplug or Misha the Olympic bear, and as he descended the stairs with a daughter clinging to each hand I conducted a kind of physical assessment in my head, to figure out if it would be better for him to be in the front or the back of the armoire while we carried it.

The front.

It wasn't all that heavy, but of course he acted like it weighed several tons, and his groupies were in heaven.

He cursed impressively with each step: "Ah! This would make a preacher swear!" "Jesus Christ on a bicycle!" "Ten thousand thundering typhoons!" "Heavens to Murgatroyd!" "Odds bodkins!" "Good Lord almighty!" "*Ay caramba*!" "Goddamn this Formica devil!" "Damn it all to kingdom come!" "Great balls of fire!" "Thunderation!"

. . . I could go on.

His daughters grew more and more scandalized at each curse, scolding him and waving their arms at him. "PAPA!"

I brought up the rear, lapping it all up—and bearing all the weight.

What would they have left for later in life, after a childhood like that? I wondered. A life of boredom, or a taste for partying? A timid stomach or a hell of a lot of chutzpah?

God knows I loved my parents, so composed, calm, and discreet, but I would have loved it so much if they'd entrusted me with this secret in addition to their affection. That happiness was found in stairwells, and that you mustn't be afraid. Afraid of making noise, afraid of being happy, afraid of disturbing the neighbors and swearing at the top of your lungs.

Afraid of life, of the future, of crisis, and of all the made-in-China Pandora's boxes that old assholes who are even more afraid than we are keep opening to discourage us so they can keep all the booty for themselves.

Yeah, maybe these little girls will become disillusioned someday; maybe they have it too good too soon and it'll all go by too fast; and maybe pretty soon they'll start to feel overpowered and weighed down by their all-powerful mini-Papa, but in the meantime . . . in the meantime . . . what wonderful memories they're storing up.

On the third-floor landing, a curious old biddy has opened her door.

"Madame Bizot! Finally, finally! There you are, Madame Bizot!" he bellows. "Maison Lévitan, delivering you the 'Marquise d'Azur' armoire you ordered from us in April 1964! Beautiful, isn't it? Excuse us, excuse us! Push, Madame Bizot, push! Now, where would you like us to put it?"

She was aghast. I laughed. I laughed, not giving a damn that I was doing all the heavy lifting and bashing a bunch of plaster off the wall while I was at it, because the passage was so narrow and he was so round that I was going to end up flat as a pancake without him even realizing it.

"Let it go," I eventually ordered, hoisting the thing onto my back. "I'll take it the rest of the way by myself; it'll be quicker that way."

"Oh . . . oh, you scoundrel. You just want to show off for my wife, is that it? Monsieur wants to flirt? The Casanova, the boy toy, the . . . the smooth operator wants his hour of glory, right?"

He didn't stop for breath until I was at their front door.

FIVE, THE MICROWAVES

I followed his wife's directions while he got dressed, bow tie included.

"This way, in the kitchen . . . near the window. Oh, it's so pretty! I love it! It's straight out of a Martine book, don't you think? Just like in *Martine fait des crêpes*. All we're missing is Patapouf!"

When I stood up, there he was, right behind me, gravely holding out his little hand:

"Isaac. Isaac Moïse. Like the tour operator in Egypt."

I felt a strong urge to giggle, but he wasn't laughing at all. Maybe this was his way of marking the start of a possible new era: after the dirty jokes . . . friendship.

"Yann," I reply, meeting his eyes. "Yann Carcarec."

"Breton?"

"Breton."

"Welcome to our home, Yann. What can I offer you to drink, to thank you for making Alice so happy?"

"Oh—thank you, no, I was just going out to see a movie."

He already had a corkscrew in his hand, and my refusal stupefied him. Worse, it left him speechless.

Alice smiled at me indulgently. She'd forgive me this first faux pas.

The little girls, on the other hand, flashed me their terrified deer-in-headlights expressions again: but . . . but . . . what about the final act?

The microwave clock read 8:37 P.M. If I ran for the metro, I could still make the film. But . . . it was winter. And I was hungry. And tired. Exhausted. And all kinds of other stuff. Could I really allow myself the luxury of flaking out on these people?

My poor little Woof-Woof handler's brain was spinning. I'd had more fun in the last ten minutes than in the last ten months of my life (and I'm only saying "months" for the sake of my dignity), and the reasons I'd wanted to see this movie again so badly—intelligence, humor, humanity—would, I had a feeling, also be offered to me if I didn't go to the film.

Yeah, but . . .

"Yann, you shouldn't think so much, my friend. It'll make you stupid."

8:38 P.M. I smiled.

He set down the bottle of red he'd been inspecting with a skeptical frown and we went down to the cellar.

I stopped at my place on the way back upstairs, to change my shirt (Alice), forget my cell phone (Mélanie), and get—for the little girls—two of the most ridiculous samples I had in stock. (A keychain that repeats your name nonstop, louder and louder, when you lose your keys, until you stop it—that is, if no one's clapped you in a straitjacket in the meantime—by throwing it furiously against a wall when you finally find it.) (That's called "planned obsolescence.")

Ha ha. Their papa's going to *love* this.

Six, the Mess

These are just details," you're thinking. Of course they are, yes, but, you know, you don't need to have gone to design school to understand the importance of details. The most moving things never jump right out at you; it's the eyes that find them, and the rest . . .

The rest is less interesting.

The almost-nothing that had made me decide to accept my neighbor's invitation to have a drink with him that night . . . it wasn't the panache of his prattling, which was absolutely the verbal equivalent of his colorful plumage; it wasn't the cold outside or the warmth of his handshake; and it wasn't, I truly believe, the prospect of eating another kebab alone standing in the street, or even the energy-sapping work of my inner demons. No; what made me decide to give myself over to the moment was when he'd said, "What can I offer you to drink, to thank you for making *Alice* so happy," rather than "for making *my wife* so happy."

After his astonishing old-fashioned/macho/misogynist/Guitry-esque display two minutes earlier in the stairwell, the fact that her first name came more naturally to his lips than a sort of . . . possessive designation . . . had filled me with awe.

It's a detail, I grant you.

One that, it so happens, I was touched by.

Another:

When I came back, their children were at the table. We

were in a kitchen full of sound and fury; it even felt as if I were walking on crunchy pasta shells.

"Have a seat in the living room; it'll be quieter. I'll join you as soon as they've finished," suggested the mistress of the house.

"Here," he said, handing her a glass of wine he'd just aerated, sniffed, and tasted with great care. "It's the Roussanne Pierrot gave us; tell me what you think. Okay, chickadees, hurry up and finish your dinner, because Mister Yann here told me he had . . . (conspiratorial wink, smiling eyes, loud stage whisper) . . . a little present for you."

When mice giggle amongst themselves, it must sound pretty much just like that.

We clinked glasses above the heads of the two little busybodies, who had been greatly calmed down by their father's announcement, even though the gift (big sigh) must be "really *very tiny*" because I "didn't have a bag." (It was the first time I'd been this close to kids, and I didn't know they had such highly-developed deductive powers.)

Alice, standing at the sink, looked at me, smiling, while her husband, seated on a stool with his back against the wall, peeled clementines for his daughters and asked me question after question about my life.

Half of me fobbed off the questions ("Do you have polka-dotted ones too?" she asked. "Dalmatian Woof-Woofs?") while the other half, in the background, promised myself: When I have a girlfriend, I'll be like him. I won't leave my wife all alone in the kitchen with the children. I won't be like every other man I know, spending my time in peace in the living room having "guy time."

That was the second detail.

"What are you thinking about, Yann? You have a dreamy look on your face."

"No—no, nothing."

I wasn't thinking about anything. I'd just remembered that I did have a girlfriend.

* * *

The wine made me tipsy. I hadn't eaten anything since morning and I was feeling pretty good. Slightly drunk, slightly cheerful, slightly off my head.

I looked and watched, asked questions and learned. For the curious person, the documentary filmmaker, the good-for-nothing dilettante, this was an absolute feast.

. . . the faded red fish, the tired ranunculus, the delicacy of the wineglass I was drinking from, the Napoleon III chairs, the big table salvaged from the refectory of an English boarding school, its dark, almost black wooden surface polished by two centuries of rolling plates and the percussive pounding of tin cutlery all along its length and breadth (a fact attested to by the little dents ringing its circumference); the little girls perched on piles of Arcturial catalogues, the weeping-willow chandeliers dripping with dun-colored wax, the Poul Henningsen ceiling light with its fashionable patina and its broken leaf (shell?), the to-do list, the unframed canvases by forgotten minor masters, the completely failed brioche of a completely failed Chardin and all those abandoned landscapes, forgotten and lost in succession, saved as one lot by Isaac and restored to the light.

More recent sketches and engravings and very beautiful pastels—and the children's drawings, stuck with magnets to the refrigerator door: a golden moon, circle-shaped hearts, and princesses with disproportionately long arms.

Fotomat strips unapproved by the Ministry of the Interior, with nobody in them, or the tip of a doll's ear in the lower right-hand corner, maybe. School memos about swimming days and the dreaded return of lice. Teapots, antique bowls, canisters of tea. Cast iron, stoneware, wicker, and turned wood. Lacquer and a bamboo whisk. Alice's passion for ceramics: Raku ware, bone china, celadon glaze, faience, porcelain, and smoke-fired ceramic.

She told me about the various items (the vitreous layer, a type of glaze with which pieces are coated at the time of firing) (uh, I think, anyway . . .) (she talked fast) (and I was pretty cooked myself!), which have a much more rustic quality in Japan because testaments to the superiority of nature over the creative power of mankind (asymmetries or irregularities caused by the Spirit of the earth, wind, sun, water, wood, or fire) were perceived as a sign of perfection, while Chinese bowls were judged on their uniformity and extraordinary smoothness.

The kilns of Ru, Jun, Longquan. This bowl "with such a fine lip," this "soft" glaze, and this one, in "jackrabbit hair." The splendors of the Song dynasty, and the especial joy of hearing Chinese civilization spoken of, rather than Chinese imports.

The stopped clock, the bird skulls sitting on a shelf between a packet of Chocapic and some jars of jam, a reproduction of a photo by Jacques-Henri Lartigue (the one of the girl who, just about a century ago, fell down and revealed her petticoats, laughing). The exhibition advertisements, invitations to private showings, and friendly little notes from gallery owners who know how to network. "Inevitably, all the money Isaac earns by selling his old-fashioned things, I give back to living artists!" The braid of heads of pink garlic, the Espelette peppers, the plump quinces, the mummified pomegranate, the ginger preserves in a silver goblet, the collection of peppers (long peppers, Kampot, and Muntok white peppercorns), the heap of fresh mint, the bunch of coriander, the bush of thyme, the wooden spoons.

The cat's dish full of fish-shaped kibble and the cat itself winding between my ankles; the overflowing garbage can, the dish towels (both clean and dirty), the cookbooks, the recipes by Olivier Roellinger and Mapie de Toulouse-Lautrec, a dietician's prescription forgotten between *La Bible de la tripe et des abats* and *Le Dictionnaire des noms de cépages en France*; the soft music, Caribbean reggae; the basket filled with almonds, which Isaac cracked and offered to each of us in turn; the taste of the cool, fruity white wine after you'd crunched down two or three of the almonds; the scent of clementines and their glow (you could turn them into little makeshift candles if you knew how to peel them correctly and pour a little olive oil on them), and the lights we turned out to admire their quivering luminescent candlelight.

The grain of their beautiful transparent orange color, the aroma of whatever was bubbling on the stove, the smell of cardamom, cloves, honey, and soy sauce mingling with meat juices, and the scent of chamomile when you leaned over the heads of the little girls to relight a reluctant candle . . .

The alabaster drops of Alice's earrings; her tiny antique watch, her loose chignon and broad neck. The stirring line of delicate vertebrae running from the bottom of her nape. Her man's shirt, monogrammed "I.M." beneath the right breast; her worn jeans, her belt buckle (simple, hammered, rustic, very Thorgal and Aaricia). The way she held her wineglass in front of her mouth and smiled at us through it; the way she laughed when her husband said something funny, and her wonderment at him, at realizing that it was still there, that it still worked, that she loved him as surely and hopelessly as the first time they met—he was just in the middle of telling me about it—in the lingerie department at La Samaritaine; he was with his poor mama, who was in despair of finding panties in her size, while she was examining some ridiculous bustier intended to stun someone other than him, and, to seduce her, he had launched into an imitation of Sophia Loren in *Heller in Pink Tights* (original *and* subtitled versions)—after bursting out of a dressing room like a jack-in-the-box . . . dressed in said pink tights.

She recounted how she had waited delicately—she only admitted this to him for the first time right then—for them to slink away before continuing to rifle shamelessly through the racks of fluff, and how, arriving at the checkout counter, she had been struck with the realization that she didn't want to salvage her relationship anymore; she only wanted to laugh again with the plump little man in the light linen suit who spoke the Yiddish of the Saint-Paul metro stop with his mother and the Italian of Aldo Maccione with her. She wanted him to perform for her, as he had promised, scenes from *Two Women* and *Sex Pot*. She had never in her life wanted anything so ferociously, so desperately. She had searched for them everywhere, run after them in the street, and—at the Quai de la Mégisserie, breathless, scarlet-faced, panting, in front of the window of a packed bird shop, she had invited him for dinner that same evening. "Son, son," the old lady had quavered, "did we forget to pay for something?" "No, Mama, no. Don't worry. It's only this young lady, who has come to ask me to marry her." "Oh, is that all? You scared me!" And she told us how, her heart still confused, she had again watched them walk away arm-in-arm, beneath the mocking gazes of dozens of jeering birds.

Every one of my senses was being appealed to, flattered, fêted. It wasn't the wine that was making me drunk; it was them. The two of them. This building-up, this game between them, the way they had of constantly interrupting each other while holding out a hand to me to haul me on board, on board with them, and make me laugh again. I loved it. I felt like a piece of frozen meat put out to thaw in the sunshine.

I couldn't remember when I'd been a part of so much witty repartee, when I'd been so open, so tender, considered so worthy of attention. Yes, I'd forgotten. Or maybe I'd never known.

I grew old and then young again; I was melting with happiness.

Of course, at some point I asked myself the natural question.

Of course I wondered if it was my presence that sharpened and inspired them so much, or if they were always this way . . . but I knew the answer: as conductive as we were, alcohol and I could never carry this much weight; what I was seeing was their life, their daily routine, the usual. I was a welcome and warmly received witness, but I was only a passing spectator, and tomorrow, in this kitchen, they would have every bit as much fun together.

I was dumbfounded.

I didn't know you could live like this. I didn't know. I was like a pauper invited into an extremely wealthy home, and I confess, along with my pleasure, I felt a rising prickle of sadness, of envy. Just a prickle. Something that hurt. I could never—would never know how to—claim all this for myself. It was too elusive.

As I listened to them and bantered endlessly with them, I was also admiring the way their daughters linked elbows beneath this umbrella that was too small for them both. They already understood that these adults would never be as interested in the two of them as they were in each other, and calmly equipped themselves so that they wouldn't suffer because of it.

They chattered to each other, laughed with each other, lived as a duo, took care of one another, and had already left the table when Isaac—who, bellowing, "Married within the year!" (gulp) as he poured the dregs of the first bottle of wine into my glass (he had chosen three, including two bottles of red, which he had uncorked and recorked and immediately returned to the cellar . . .)—chuckled in his beard as he listened, maybe for the thousandth time, to the end of the beginning of their story.

So he had accepted Alice's invitation and entertained her for the whole evening—but not only that; he had affected and intrigued her as well, and then walked her back to his place (it was difficult at hers; a cuckold-in-training had taken to spying through the peephole) before suddenly taking his leave by standing on tiptoe to kiss her on the cheek.

"Alice, my little Alice," he had said, holding her long-fingered hands tightly in his short-fingered ones, "I'd rather warn you right away: it won't be an easy match. I'm forty-five years old, an old man, and I still live with my mother . . . but trust me, the day I introduce her to you, we'll bring our baby along, and she'll be much too busy looking for a resemblance to me to chastise you for not being Jewish." She had bent her knees to offer him her other cheek, and everything had happened exactly as he predicted . . . except that all these years later— that is, tonight—she still hadn't recovered! Her expression mocking, hands clasped, she reenacted the crazy scene for me, imitating the sudden gravity of his voice: "Alice . . . my little Alice . . . it won't be an easy match," and laughed, as we clinked glasses to her memory of the memory of this sweet madness.

Madeleine and Misia (I discovered their first names at the same time as the "mode of use" of my gift) had basically climbed up me like a mountain, and listened to me silently.

"See, you push this button . . . the little mouth, there . . . and when the green light comes on, you record your first name. Or whatever you want, really. Now imagine what your keychain would say to you if it was really calling you. For example: 'Misia! Find me!' or 'Madeleine! Here I am!' and then you press the same button again, like that, and when you lose it you clap, and it'll say exactly what you recorded. Handy, right?"

"And then what?"

"Then . . . uh, then . . . well, I don't know. Then you just test them out! Each of you can record whatever she wants, and give it to her sister, who will hide it the very best she can, and the first one who finds her keychain wins!"

(Hey, I'm pretty good with kids, right? Too goddamn bad I never came back.)

"Wins what?"

"The cat-o'-nine-tails . . . " intoned their father spookily, " . . . the cat-o'-nine-tails, and two bloody behinds!"

And the little mice scurried away, shrieking loudly.

I don't remember how we got on the subject, but we were in the middle of discussing Brazilian architecture of the '50s and '60s; Caldas, Tenreiro, Sergio Rodrigues, etc., while Isaac (who knew everything about everything, and knew everyone, and never said anything unoriginal, and—and this was the most refreshing thing of all—never talked about money, or speculations, or sales records, or any of those boastful anecdotes that generally fill discussions about art, and design in particular) was handing me plates and glasses which I arranged awkwardly in their dishwasher when, suddenly, metallic, nasal salvos of "Wiener fart!" and "Butt fart!" were heard from the depths of the hallway, echoing more and more and more AND EVEN MORE LOUDLY throughout the apartment.

Scato, allegro, crescendo, vivacissimo!

The keychains were apparently well-hidden, and the little darlings much too overstimulated to take the trouble of finding them.

They clapped their hands, listened for a response, and laughed hysterically, cheering at the consistency and obstinacy of their big Asian parrots, which obliged them even more loudly.

Alice snorted with laughter because her daughters were as silly as she was, while Isaac shook his head hopelessly, in despair over being the only male trapped in this gymnasium of ridiculous females, and I couldn't believe my ears: how could such angelic beings, with such tiny bodies and such crystalline little voices, produce such booming laughter?

* * *

There was no question of my staying for dinner. What I mean is, the question wasn't even asked. On a white table-cloth which Alice smoothed, leaning in my direction (ahhh . . . the sound, the touch of her palm on the linen . . . and the gaping of her blouse . . . and the . . . the silky sheen of her bra . . . and . . . oh, my heart . . . how it crumbled into pieces . . .) . . . ahem, anyway, on the tablecloth, Isaac arranged three place settings, still talking to me about the Brasilia of Oscar Niemeyer as he had experienced it in 1976.

He reminisced about the cathedral, its size, its acoustics, and the absence of God, too intimidated and lost in there; he found the bread and sliced it, describing the Supreme Court and the government ministries, asking me if he should put out soup plates, regretted not going into the Place du Colonel-Fabien, offered to be my tour guide there one day, and shook out a clean napkin for me.

Instead of being his wife's lover, I could have been his son . . .

"You're tired," he said suddenly. "I'm boring you silly with all my stories, aren't I?"

"Not at all! Not at all! Quite the opposite!"

If I was rubbing my eyes like that it wasn't because I was sleepy, but to dry my tears on the sly.

Unsuccessfully.

And the more I rubbed, the more the tears came.

Stupid.

I made a joke of it. I said it was the wine. That my wine tasted of sea air and salt. The fault—really—of the scent of granite that consumes your soul, the outdoor crosses, the votive offerings, the spring tides. The famous *saudade* of the Côtes-d'Armor . . .

I wasn't fooling anyone, of course. It was just that I had

thawed out completely by that time . . . and in doing so I leaked a little water. That's all.

Move along, move along. Nothing to see here. Everyone gets screwed over by his soul every now and then, right? That son of am bitch of a little thought bubble that rises up without warning to remind you that your life doesn't measure up, and that you're lost in your absurd dreams, which are much too grand for you. If that doesn't happen to you, you've given up. Or, even better, much better and much easier, you've never felt the need to measure yourself against . . . I don't know . . . to hold yourself accountable, to look yourself up and down. God, how I envied those people. And the further I went, the more I felt like they—other people—were almost all like that, and I was the fool. Like I was just listening to myself piss on dead leaves.

But that isn't my style, I'm sure of it. I don't like to complain. I wasn't at all like that when I was little. The thing is that I don't know where I am in my life. And I don't mean in *life*, I mean in *my* life. My age, my purposeless youth, my degree that impresses no one, my bullshit job, Mélanie's sixty points, her fake cheek kisses that flicker in the empty air, my parents . . . My parents, who I don't dare call anymore, who don't dare call me, who have always been so very present, and who have nothing left to offer me for the moment except their discretion.

It's horrible.

Diversion:
Once, when I'd gone with her to visit her son's grave (my mother's older brother, the last deep-sea fisherman in the family), my granny Saint-Quay explained to me that you could recognize happiness by the sound it made as it left. I must have been ten or eleven, and my knife and shackle wrench had just been stolen, and I got the message loud and clear.

With love, it's the opposite. Love, you recognize by the

mess it makes when it turns up. For example, for me, all it took was a kind, funny, cultivated man, a neighbor I barely knew, to set a glass and a plate and a knife and fork in front of me, for me to break apart from head to toe.

It was as if this man had pushed a wedge into my most secret breach, and was slowly opening me up, an enormous crank in his hand.

Love.

Suddenly, I understood Alice. I understood why she had panicked so much on that first day at La Samaritaine, when she had looked up and believed she had lost him forever. I understand why she had taken off running like a crazy person, and all but tackled him in the street.

That violence with which she had caught his arm—it wasn't to force him to turn around; it was because she was grabbing on to him. And that was what brought me to tears, that gesture. Terra firma.

"Alice, my dear . . . this boy is starving to death."

"The girls have school tomorrow; I should put them to bed first," she grimaced.

In the distance, moments of quiet (recording sessions) alternated with bursts of pure madness (hide-and-seek on the last day of school and other wild exclamations like something off an African savannah).

"*Would have had* school," she corrected herself. "Well, let's sit down, then. I have a pumpkin soup with chestnuts that should restore our handsome Breton's spirits . . . *joli Breton; poil au téton!*"

It was as if an angel had become tarnished and been cast out of heaven.

"Oh, please, you two! Don't look at me like that! Surely I have the right to regress a little too, don't I?"

*

Isaac told me where to find the bathroom, and I went to wash my hands.

Aside from the little girls' room at the end of the hallway, which was pink and sparkly, the rest of their apartment—what I could see of it, at least—was empty. No carpets, no furniture, no lamps or curtains or anything else, and bare walls.

It made an odd impression, as if life on this planet was completely restricted to their kitchen.

"Are you moving?" I asked, unfolding my napkin.

No, no, it was just to rest the eyes. They had an old country place in the South to which they escaped as often as possible, which was stuffed to the gills with all kinds of sentimental bric-a-brac, but here, outside the kitchen, they didn't want anything to remind Isaac of his job.

"A bedroom for the girls, a kitchen for the family, a sofa for music, and a bed for love!" he crowed.

Alice explained that she was fine with it, understood it, appreciated it. And that she had a marvelous bed. Immense. A king-size.

(A king-size . . .) (This woman had the gift of eroticizing everything as if it were nothing at all.) (It was exhausting.) (Etymologically speaking.) (It was backbreaking.)

* * *

The glitter of the candles, the velvetiness of the soup, the crumb of the bread, the filet mignon, the wild rice, the homemade chutney, the wine . . . this wine, that warmed you little by little, that breathed so much life into you by relieving you of the burden of so much of yourself; that . . . turned your soul transparent. The bursts of the little girls' voices, coming farther and farther apart and more and more quietly (there was nothing accidental about that, according to their mother) (they were trying to be inconspicuous because they thought we'd forgotten about them, naturally) (could this be possible?) (were little girls already this wily at such a young age?) (no) (come on) (leave me with a few illusions, please, Mr. Heartbreak . . .), the flow of our conversation, our laughs, provocations, debates, disagreements and agreements. I already knew I wouldn't remember any of it (I would be—was already—much too tipsy), but I also knew I'd never forget any of it either. I knew this evening would be my cursor, my Jesus Christ. That from now on there would be a before and an after, and that Alice and Isaac—and it was still very confusing, but there it was, and it was the only thing I was sure of in that haze of alcohol and well-being—had become my benchmark.

And I was already afraid.

I could already tell that this was going to be an insurmountable hangover.

In the chaos, jumping from one subject to the next and then to dessert, we talked about her work (dance instructor) (so that was it . . .) (. . . what a beautiful body she must have . . .), about Michael Jackson and Carolyn Carlson, about Pina Bausch and Dominique Mercy and the Place du Châtelet, and Broadway and Suresnes and Stanley Donen (I asked her to pass me the water, the bread, the pepper, the salt, the butter, and who knows what else, for the simple pleasure of watching her arm unfold and stretch), about her mother, a pianist in a conservatory of classical dance, who had spent the best years of her life watching her little ballet pupils fly away, and who had died last year lamenting the "clumsy" performance of her "final fugue"; about cancer, about illness, about the Institut Gustave-Roussy and the great merit of its doctors and the nurses whom no one ever mentioned; about those times in life when grief seizes you without warning; the green heavens of childhood that were never really that green, about Heaven, period; God, his mysteries and contradictions, the film I was going to see this evening, that unforgettable scene where the parents resolve to lose sight of their son in order to free him from the weight of being their son. About my parents, and the ancient car my father had been lovingly restoring (off and on) for more than forty years, and which he had promised to finish for my sister's wedding; about my sister, who had gotten divorced since then, and my niece, who, all of a sudden one day, had taken onto her slender, tattooed shoulders the great hopes of Papy and his Fiat Balilla beribboned in white. About the neighborhood, the local businesses, the baker who always spoke so rudely to us and who, when she turned around, could often be seen with white flour handprints on her large round ass. We talked about school, and music, which children never learn at the age when they need it most and when it would be easiest for them to learn while having fun at the same time; about what a waste that was, and the revolutions you had to have the courage to lead (Alice told me how she and one of her friends, a percussionist, went into nursery schools and day-cares once a week to let the littlest ones play with instruments—a triangle, a little guiro, maracas—and added that there was nothing more comforting in the world than watching a baby's eyes open wide when a rain stick swished in its ear). About Isaac's theory that life, and I needed to remember this, hung by the slenderest of threads—he had come to understand this very young, at the age of reason, let's say, when he was ordered to spell out his last name, and around him—always, and no matter where he was—the light changed depending on whether he put one or two dots above the *i*, and the cynicism, the recoil, and finally the strength that a revelation like that had put into his body, a single dot, one dot or two. For a child it was dizzying. We spoke about the *ballets russes*, Stravinsky, Diaghilev; about their cat who had been given to them by their neighbors in the South, and who had a

southern accent when it meowed. We talked about the difference between the Chamonix biscuits of our childhood and the
ones you could get today, and the same thing was true of
Figolu cookies. Was it we or the recipe that had changed?
About Mansart, and the Prince de Ligne, and cabinetry, and
ironworking, and the books published by Editions Vial, and
Bauhaus, and the little Calder circus, and the signage system
in the Berlin metro.

Among other things.

The rest is a bit hazy.

At one point, Alice left us to put the little girls to bed, and
I couldn't stop myself from asking my host if it was true. If
their story, the one they had just told me, was true. The way
they'd met, and all that.

"Sorry?"

"No, I mean . . . " I babbled, "you . . . did you really talk to
her about a child that first night? In front of your door? Even
though you barely knew her?"

What a beautiful smile he gave me then. His eyes disappeared, and every hair in his beard wiggled with pleasure. He
stroked the hairs to calm them down, leaned forward, and said
to me, low:

"Yann, my young friend . . . Of course I knew her. You
don't *meet* the people you love; you *recognize* them. Didn't you
know that?"

"Uh . . . no."

"Then I'll teach you." His face darkened, and he stared into
the depths of his glass. "You see, when I met Alice, I . . . I was a
very sick man. I really was forty-five years old, really an old man,
and I really lived with my parents. With my mother, that is. Let's
see . . . how can I explain this to you? Are you a gambler?"

"Pardon?"

"I'm not talking about Pope Joan or craps. I mean suffering, addiction. Games with winnings and a capital G: casino, poker, horse racing . . . "

"No."

"Then I highly doubt you'll be able to understand."

He set his glass down on the table and continued, without meeting my eyes again:

"I was . . . a hunter. Or a dog, rather. Yes, a dog. A hunting dog. Always restless, always on the alert, always howling, scratching, ferreting in corners. Obsessed by the idea of seeking and destroying, of tracking, of fetching. You can't imagine who I was, Yann—or *what* I was, I should say. You can't imagine. I could go thousands of kilometers at a time without sleeping; I could skip meals and keep myself from pissing for whole days. I could cross Europe on a hunch, on the idea of a stamp or a signature of the vague promise of maybe, just maybe, the arch of a back like this or a way of painting clouds like that. The certainty that there was, in Poland or Vierzon or Anvers or I don't know where, a veneer to scratch or a false ceiling to remove or a drapery to lift. Thousands and thousands of kilometers to realize at the first glance that I'd been wrong, and that I had to leave again—quick!—because I'd already lost too much time, and someone might beat me out for another opportunity if I stayed even one second longer!"

Silence.

"I lost sleep, decency, the awareness of other living people. They say hunters have a taste for blood; well, when I gritted my teeth, what I tasted was the dust of auction rooms, the odors of wax and varnish, tapestries and old horsehair. And sweat and fear and those silent little farts that mean someone has a terrible case of the runs, and the awful funky breath of all those old nutcases that lose their minds over a titian-haired portrait but let their own teeth rot away in their mouths. What I tasted was the smell of diesel from the tailpipes of trucks, and of banknotes quickly counted and stuffed in a pocket, and grieving households, and families at war, and visits to hellish hospices and castles in dire straits, defeated and sad and soon to be stripped of everything. What I tasted was death, the kind that hovered over certain private mansions, and certain amateurs I knew, and certain collectors who, I knew, knew me. The cries of auctioneers and the dry crack of the hammer, the auction sales, death announcements in the daily report, the confidences that were sometimes dropped along with the cigar ashes, the Savoyard rooms, the hours spent around tables with old country notaries. Reading the *Gazette* while driving to save time. The power struggles with the haulage contractors, the mafia of experts, the planes, the trade shows, the biennials . . . I don't know if you read stories about trappers or poachers or Sioux hunters when you were a little boy, Yann. All those unbelievable stories of hunting and tracking and safaris. Ahab and his whale, Huston and his elephant, Eichmann and his Jews. Did you read those things?"

"No."

"All of them were very sick people. Like me."

He smiled then, and met my eyes again.

After pouring us each a little more wine, which we were nursing at this point rather than really drinking, he continued:

"My great-grandfather was a merchant; my grandfather was a merchant, and so were my uncle and my father, and his offspring after him. The crazy Moïses—foxhounds, all of them, all down the line! (Laughter.) Do you know why my uncle came back from the camps? Because he wanted to bring a Bohemian crystal ashtray to his fiancée. He could barely lift it, and he didn't survive long, but he came back with it! And when I met Alice, I was at that point too. I was also a ghost, nothing but skin and bones with a fixed stare, already dead—but who brought the shit back, goddammit! Who never came back empty-handed!"

Silence. Long silence.

"And then?" I ventured, to steer him back on track.

"Then? Nothing. Then, Alice."

Teasing smile.

"Come now, neighbor, come now . . . don't look at me like a shocked choirboy. I told you I had an eye. An unfailing eye. And I saw the way you looked at her on the landing when she came out behind me; I saw it! Honestly, what can I tell you about her that you haven't already seen and loved?"

He had asked the question very gently, and I bit my lip so I wouldn't cry again.

Because of the standing stones of Pergat, high percentages, my Opinel knife, and this whole thing.

Overwhelming.

Fortunately—or maybe it was out of delicacy—he'd gone back to speechifying:

"You know, it was a major challenge for my mother to find panties that she liked! Girdle panties, that's what she wanted, I remember. Which means that I had time to observe this young woman—a dancer, I could tell—surreptitiously, while she looked at lingerie that was more and more luscious, and assessed each item, knitting her brows, as if they were cartridges or gunpowder. Her solemnity intrigued me, and her neck . . . ah . . . her neck, the way she carried her head, her style . . . Of course, she eventually sensed me looking at her. She looked up, and looked at me, and looked at my mother, and then looked at me again, and she smiled at us gently, while hurriedly dropping her little bits of lace as if afraid of shocking us. And there, Yann, right there, in that second, I died and came back to life. Some would call that a cliché, right? Some would say I'm just being romantic, but I'm telling you, because you'll understand, and because I already love you, that it's the pure truth. Off/On. I came apart and was put back together in one flutter of her eyelashes."

After the almonds, he peeled clementines for me, too. He

inspected each segment and delicately peeled off all the white strings before lining them up single-file around my plate.

"Then," he sighed, "then I said to myself, oh, you big lug, a pretty little thing like that won't come around twice. And my ancient Moïse blood, mine and the blood of three generations of rabbit hunters, didn't have to think twice. If this dream of a woman passed right under my nose and I let myself get beaten to the punch, there'd be nothing left for me to do but bow out. But how to go about it? How? She was already turning away, and my mother, *oy*, was already starting to mutter the *kaddish* she reserved for bad days, cursing her worthless son, the size of her rear end, and the Eternal. I was frantic! Which is where the pink tights come in, because something I've learned in my career, and this applies to any occasion where fate comes into play that way, I would think . . . there comes a time when you have to give destiny a bit of a nudge. And by that I mean you have to take the initiative. Yes. There always comes a time when you have to go grab luck by the scruff of the neck and try to steer it in your direction by staking everything you've got on it. All the chips, all the cash, everything that can be bid on. Your comfort, your pension, the respect of your peers, your dignity, *everything*. In a case like this it isn't 'God helps those who help themselves,' it's 'Make God laugh and maybe he'll reward you.' I came out of that dressing room like I was playing a hand of poker, like I was putting my life on the table, *just to see*, and I launched into a ridiculous imitation of Sophia Loren—being very careful to avoid the appalled face of my mother, who was clinging to the plastic thighs of an Eminence mannequin so she wouldn't keel right over. My goddess laughed, and I thought I was victorious—but no. She was still looking at garter belts."

He broke off and smiled.

We could hear snatches of Alice's voice in the distance, at the end of the hall, reading a story to the girls.

"I mean, what was I expecting to happen? She was so young and beautiful, and I was so old and ugly. And I looked like such an idiot! Wearing panties! Panties under pink tights, with my gnarly, hairy little Louis XV hooves! What was I expecting? To bewitch her? So I got dressed again, vanquished but not despairing. After all, I'd made her laugh. Besides, the best players of the game of Chance share this quality: we like to win, but we also know how to lose. A true gambler is a good sport."

He got up, filled the kettle, and put it on to boil before continuing:

"I was out in the street with my pain-in-the-ass mother hanging on to my arm and the memory of my beautiful ballerina before my eyes, and I . . . I was sad. Yes, I had died and come back to life, but frankly, I was wondering *why*, since my new life seemed much less fun than the old one. And my mother was still there, on top of it! But mostly I was annoyed. The underwear she'd wanted hadn't fit at all. With a body like that she could squeeze herself into silk or cotton, but not that horrible nylon, you see. I sighed and distracted myself from old Jacqueline's whining by imagining what pretty chemises and other lingerie I would have draped *her* in, if she had let me love her, and . . . well, I was lost in these agonizing daydreams when I lost my balance, and would you believe it, there she was, out of nowhere, grabbing my arm so hard she almost wrenched it out of the socket, the crazy woman!"

As he poured boiling water into an old teapot filled with lime-blossom tea leaves, he unleashed his second-most beautiful smile of the evening.

"You're lucky," I murmured.

"It's true. I am. Though women's tights are bloody difficult to put on . . . "

"I didn't mean only you, I meant the two of you. You're both lucky."

"Yes."

Silence.

"Listen. Since it's you," he continued, "since it's you, and since it's now, I'm going to confess something to you that I've never had the guts to tell anyone before. Of course, my mother is still alive, of course. Since I was born she's been haranguing me about her imminent death. When I was little she traumatized me with it, and she's spent my whole adult life blackmailing me emotionally with her phony 'this is it's, and now I'm sure she'll outlive me. She'll outlive us all. And that's fine. But she's an old lady now. A very old lady, who can barely walk, and she's deaf, and she can hardly see anymore. But none of that keeps the Eternal from fixing her right up every Thursday, you see. Every Thursday I take her to lunch in a little bistro downstairs from her flat, and every Thursday, after the coffee, we go through the same ritual; we walk with tiny little steps to the Allée des Justes, near the Pont Louis-Philippe. We stroll, we dawdle, we practically crawl, and she hangs onto my arm, and I support her . . . hold her up . . . carry her, almost. Her legs hurt, her rheumatism's practically making a martyr out of her; her neighbors are killing her; her home-care worker's about to finish her off, the new mailman is making her crazy, the TV is poisoning her, this world is persecuting her, and this time, *this* time, it's *definitely* over, she's done for. This time she can feel it; this time, my dear, I'm really going to die, you know. And I've been taking her word for it for ages now! But when we get there she stops complaining, and finally shuts up. She shuts up because she's waiting for me to tell her, again, the names of all the human beings engraved there in the stone. The first *and* last names. Of course I do it every Thursday, and while I'm filling her ears with this little laic litany, I can feel—physically feel—the weight on my forearm getting lighter. Touched, all at once, her gaze softened, and with an angelic smile, my old Jacquot stands up a little straighter and perks back up. And there, exactly like on a mobile phone screen, I can see them. I can see, in her cataract-whitened pupils, the little bars of her internal battery, more and more bars the more names I read. And then after a minute she remembers that her legs hurt, and we leave as slowly as we came. Just as slowly, but much more valiantly! Because these people existed, and because they did what they did, my God, it must have been hard, but . . . for them, and especially for me, she wanted to try to stay alive for just one more week. And you see, for me, Alice's voice has exactly the same effect."

Silence.

What can you say, after that?

I don't know about you, but I kept my mouth shut.

"But you know, the real key to happiness, I believe, is to laugh. To laugh together. When Gabrielle—Alice's *maman*—passed away, it was terrible because I couldn't make my beloved laugh anymore. I'd never been so unhappy in my life—and believe me, I come from a family that knows something about unhappiness! I was simple; I was raised on herring, and not even a whole lot of that. But here, I'd tried everything. She smiled, yes, but she didn't laugh anymore. Fortunately," he added, wriggling with pleasure like a young girl, "fortunately, I had one last secret up my sleeve . . . "

"What did you do?"

"Secret, Yann, *secret* . . . " he intoned in a voice of exaggerated mysteriousness.

"What are you telling him now?" asked Alice anxiously, having just rejoined us. "Go and kiss the girls in a minute. You too, Yann. They're demanding you, believe it or not."

Oh . . .

How proud that made me.

"But be careful," she added, raising her index finger. "No more nonsense tonight, okay?"

When we went into their room, the littler one was already

asleep, and Madeleine was only waiting for us to kiss her before she dropped off too.

"You know what I have to do, to be allowed to kiss my daughters?" he grumbled, straightening up.

"No."

"I have to wash my beard with baby shampoo and then rub some kind of fake vanilla-smelling conditioner into it. Isn't that the most absurd thing! You see what I have to put up with?"

I smiled.

"Somehow I can't feel too sorry for you, Isaac."

"And see, now you don't feel sorry for me!"

When we got back to the kitchen, Alice was holding a steaming cup.

She kissed her husband on the forehead to thank him for thinking of her, before announcing that she was sorry to leave us but that she was tired, and dreaming of going to lie down.

(She didn't say "going to bed," she said "lie down," which knocked me out again.) (And as if that wasn't enough, at the time she said it, she pulled a long hairpin out of her chignon and shook out her hair, and, oh . . . this was another Alice . . . Alice with her hair down.) (Softer and less awe-inspiring.) (Already naked, in a manner of speaking.) (And as I mumbled "oh" and "uh" and "um" and I don't know what else even more obvious, I felt the mocking gaze of her lover drilling between my shoulder blades.)

I think she was waiting for me to kiss her, but since I felt much too rattled to lean forward any further, she ended by holding out her hand.

(Which I shook, and which was very warm.)

(Uh . . . because of the tea, I imagine.)

Even though I had no desire to leave, the few manners the alcohol had preserved inside me made me move halfheartedly toward my jacket and the road to purgatory.

"Oh, Yann," wheedled Isaac, "you're not going to leave me to do the dishes all by myself?"

God, I loved this colorful little Misha.

I loved him.

"Come on. Sit back down. Besides, you haven't even finished your clementine! What kind of wastefulness is that?!"

* * *

Alice, on her way to bed, had turned out all the lights so that we were in a kitchen illuminated only by the gleam of the candles now, and by the dimmer glow, like a memory, of the city lights filtering through the window.

We stayed that way, without speaking, for a long moment. We emptied our glasses as slowly as possible and reflected on everything we'd just experienced. We were both a little bit drunk, and slouched a little in the dark. He had resumed his place on the stool with his back against the wall, and I had turned my chair forty-five degrees so I could imitate him. We listened to the sounds of a pretty woman going through her nightly ablutions and we daydreamed.

We must probably have been thinking the same thing: that we'd just had a very nice time, and that we were lucky. At least, that's what I was thinking. And also that she brushed her teeth a little too fast, didn't she?

"How old are you?" he asked me, out of the blue.

"Twenty-six."

"I'd never seen you before. I knew the old lady who used to live in your apartment, but she moved to the country, I think."

"Yeah, she was the great-aunt of . . . of a friend. We moved into the apartment in October."

Silence.

"You're twenty-six years old and you're living in the apartment of the great-aunt of a young woman whose first name you still haven't mentioned"

He pronounced the words in a voice completely without inflection or punctuation. It sounded terrible in my ear.

I didn't answer.

"A young woman with no first name, but with very definite ideas about the cleanliness of the courtyard and the storing of strollers under the staircase."

Ah . . . we were definitely talking about the same person.

It was said without irony or aggressiveness. It was said, that's all. I reached for my glass, because my throat had suddenly gone slightly dry.

"Yann?"

"Yes."

"What's her name, your girlfriend?"

"Mélanie."

"Mélanie. Welcome, Mélanie . . . " he murmured, addressing some phantom lost between the oven and the sink. "Well, since you're here, I have to tell you—young lady who's always in a bit of a hurry—that fussing about garbage bins and the poorly-coiled garden hose . . . it doesn't matter. And strollers and scooters under the staircase, well, they don't really matter, either. Can you hear me, Mélanie? Instead of calling the property management company every four mornings and wasting their time with these pointless little complaints, come and have a drink with us."

He raised his glass in the half-light and added:

"Because, you know, we're all going to die, Mélanie. All of us. We're all going to die one day."

I closed my eyes.

We'd had too much to drink. And I didn't need to hear all that. I didn't want to hear bad things said about Mélanie, I knew that. And I didn't want to see Isaac fall off his pedestal. I loved him.

I looked down.

"Yann, why are you letting me badmouth the woman who shares your life without coming to her defense? I'm only an old dickhead, after all. Why aren't you telling me to go to hell?"

I didn't speak. I didn't like the turn our conversation had taken, at all. I didn't want to mix my private life with all the beautiful things we'd just talked about, I didn't want to talk about myself, I didn't want to hear the words "property management company" or "garbage bin" in the mouth of a man who'd made me dream so much up to that point. To get myself out of this tight spot, I took the risk of being hurtful, too.

"Because I'm polite."

Silence.

I don't know what he was thinking, but I tried with all my might to get back to where I was by pouring us the last of the wine in the bottle, sharing it equally between our two glasses. He didn't thank me. I'm not even sure he was aware of it

I wasn't so happy anymore. I wanted a cigarette. I wanted to open the window and let the cold air distract us a little. But I didn't dare do that either, so I drank.

I couldn't look at him now. I looked at the candles. I played with the melted wax like I did as a kid. I let it harden on my fingertip and touched my lip, in the little angel's groove. It had the same lukewarmness, the same smell, the same softness as it always had.

He folded his hands, one on top of the other.

It really was time for me to go. My neighbor was a sad drunk, and I'd reached my saturation point. I'd taken in too much emotion. I was collecting myself emotionally—head, arms, legs, keys, jacket, stairs, bed, coma—when it fell, suddenly, like the blade of a very gentle guillotine:

"You can fail in life, out of politeness."

His eyes sought mine, and we stared at each other for a moment. I played the innocent and he was the persecutor, but of course I was the one who seemed nastier. Why was he telling me this?

"Why are you telling me this?"

"Because of the dodos."

Okay. He was drunk as a skunk.

"Sorry?"

"The dodos. You know, the big birds with the hooked beaks that lived on Mauritius, the ones our ancestors wiped out."

Okay, so it was WWF time now.

He continued:

"There was no reason for those poor birds to keep away from us. Their meat was bad, there was nothing interesting about their songs or their plumage, and they were so ugly that no court in Europe would have wanted them. And yet they disappeared, all the same. All of them. They'd been there since the dawn of time, and in barely sixty years, progress wiped them completely off the face of the earth. And do you know why, my little Yann?"

I shook my head.

"For three reasons. One, because they were polite. They weren't ferocious and came willingly up to people. Two, because they couldn't fly; their little wings were ridiculous and totally useless. And three, because they didn't protect their nests, and left their eggs and babies at the mercy of predators. There you go. Three flaws, and they're gone. There's only one left."

Uh . . . what could I say? The extermination of *Dodolus*

mauritius at 1:10 in the morning, as recounted by my pocket prophet . . . I'll admit, I wasn't expecting that.

He pulled his stool up to the table and bent toward me.

"Yann?"

"Mm-hmm . . . "

"Don't let them destroy you."

"What?"

"Protect yourself. Protect your nest."

What nest? I groaned inwardly. *Great-Aunt Berthaud's eighty square meters, two floors down?*

I must have snickered too loudly, because he heard me.

"Obviously I don't mean Aunt Ursula's apartment."

Silence.

"What are you talking about, then, Isaac?"

"You. Your nest is you. What you are. You have to protect it. If you don't, who will do it for you?"

And because I didn't understand his words, he continued more clearly, in "try again" mode:

"You're beautiful, Yann. You're very beautiful. And I'm not talking about your youth or your mane of hair or your large clear eyes; I'm talking about the wood you're made of. It's my job to recognize beautiful things, you know. To recognize them and determine their value. I don't make the rounds of auction rooms anymore; I'm the person people call from all over the world, the one they listen religiously to. Not because I'm so clever, but because I *know*. I know the value of everything."

"Oh yeah? And how much am I worth, according to you?"

I regretted my tone immediately. What a little asshole I was. But my guilt was pointless, because he didn't seem to have heard me.

"I'm talking about your expression, your curiosity, your kindness. The way you made everyone in my house love you in less time than it takes to say it, the way you bounced my daughters on your knees and fell madly in love with my lover without once imagining trying to steal her from me. I'm talking about the attention you pay to details, things, people. What they confide to you and what they hide from you. What you confide to them and what you hide from them. That's the first time I've heard Alice mention her mother since she died, the first time she's remembered her alive and in good health. Thanks to you, Yann, thanks to you, Gabrielle came back tonight and played a few notes of Schubert for us. I didn't dream that, did I? You heard it too?"

His eyes glittered in the dark.

"You heard it, didn't you?"

I assured him that yes, of course I had, so he would let it drop. Okay . . . I'm fine . . . I wasn't going to start crying for a woman I'd never even met . . .

"I'm talking about the tenderness with which you talk about what you love, and protect what belongs to you; I'm talking about our deliveries, which you bring upstairs every week, and the pieces of cardboard you've been wedging in the double doors since it got so cold outside, which I take out every morning so you won't get chewed out by the other residents. I'm talking about your squashed toes, your exhausted, famished big-boy tears, your obsessive, tedious work, your smiles, your discretion, your clearheadedness, and finally your politeness, which I insult, but which holds up the walls of our civilization, as I'm well aware. I'm talking about your elegance, Yann. Yes—your elegance. Don't let them destroy all of that, or what will be left of you? If you, and the people like you, don't protect your nests, then . . . what . . . what will become of this world? (Silence.) Do you understand what I'm saying?"

" . . . "

"Are you crying? But . . . but why? Is it making you cry, what I said? Come, now . . . it's not such a bad thing to be worth so much, is it?"

"Screw you, Moïse."

He jumped up and gave a delighted chortle that woke up the red fish.

"You're right, son, you're right! Here"—he thumped his glass against mine—"to our loves!"

We clinked and drank, smiling into each other's eyes.

"This wine of yours is good stuff," I said finally. "Really good stuff."

Isaac nodded, glanced at the bottle, and looked unhappy.

"Here, now I'll give you a proper reason to cry . . . those people on the label, Pierre and Ariane Cavanès, are the human beings Alice and I admire most in the whole world. Our garden in the Vallée de l'Hérault ends where their vineyard begins. It's not a big vineyard—barely thirty hectares—but every year their wine wins a bigger prize, and you'll see, one day it'll be counted among the greats. Pierre's father was a geologist and his mother had a little property, and in the 1980s, even though there was nothing there and nobody thought it was anything—not the winemakers in the region and not the professional experts—he took the risk of following his instincts and planting, there in that wild valley, some Cabernet-Sauvignon vines that had more or less fallen off the back of a truck belonging to a big winemaker in Le Médoc, if I remember correctly . . . anyway, they built a storehouse and a fermenting room, went into debt up into their eyeballs, asked the advice of a retired oenologist, and . . . you remember what Alice told us earlier about the great ceramic artists? That half-mad obsession with tests and attempts and every possible combination of water and fire, and air and earth? Well, I believe it's kind of the same thing with wine, except with fruit instead of fire, and . . . "

Isaac was exhausting me.

Stories, anecdotes, technical terms, viticultural procedures, fermentation, maceration, oak casks. Ariane, who had come from her native Normandy twenty years earlier to work the grape harvest one summer because she dreamed of running off to Bolivia and who had never left. Their love story, their fatigue, their sacrifices and their fragility; the weather, which could destroy a whole year's work in a few seconds. Unforgettable tastings, unforgettable meals, guides, notes, rankings, the recognition that was finally arriving now. Their three children, who had been strictly raised in the open air and in grape baskets, their hopes, and finally their despair.

An uninterrupted stream of verbiage from which I picked out the words "immense courage," "life of hard work," "extraordinary success," and "multiple sclerosis."

"He wants to sell," concluded Isaac. "He wants to sell everything, and even though I find that upsetting, I understand it. For me, if anything happened to Alice, I couldn't go on either. That's why Pierre and I understand each other so well. We talk big, we beat our chests and are horrible little pests, but we belong to a woman . . . "

Well, too bad for them, but the dodos have taken one more hit. We didn't care about them anymore. A lead weight had just settled on our shoulders. The candles sputtered, and my host stared off into space, lost in his own little world.

Alone, sad, unknown, hunched over.

I looked at my glass. How many swallows left? Three? Four?

Almost nothing.

Almost nothing, and what remained of one of the most beautiful evenings of my unpromising existence.

I didn't have the heart to empty it.

My offering.

My offering to the spirits watching over the unknown Ariane.

I hoped they would be grateful to me, and let her live in peace.

I reached for my jacket.

Seven, the Descent

I'm not sure how many steps separated their apartment from mine, but I was sober by the second one.

A witness, if there had been one, would have said I was lying; that he'd seen me and I was staggering, and holding onto the banister before daring to extend a foot into the void.

He was so trashed, the witness would have added, *that he ended up pressing himself against the wall and sliding along it until he reached his door.*

The dirty snitch.

If I did hesitate, it was because I really was tumbling through the void, and I wasn't pressed against the wall; I was clutching the wall in my arms. Trying to warm it up so as not to go home alone. To take it into my bed. This wall, which I had banged into so often a few hours and a lifetime earlier, holding a little marquise against my heart in the company of a baronet and two princesses, this wall, which had echoed with all the spirit and gaiety in the stairwell, so many booming curses, laughter, and childish consternation; this wall, which so stubbornly refused to come have a last drink in my apartment with me, had become my last friend. A companion as lost as I was, against whose shoulder I could slump for just a little longer before I had to go back and face real life, the real Yann, real denial.

And even admitting that this gentleman is right, Madam Judge; even admitting that, let me just say that it wasn't for very long. I'd hardly set foot into my house, finally home . . . in my girlfriend's house, her crazy old aunt's house . . . I'd hardly pushed the door of the place open when I sobered up in an instant.

I groped for the light switch. The light was ugly. I hung my jacket on a peg and the peg was ugly. And the mirror, too. The mirror was ugly. The mirror, the framed poster, the carpet, the sofa, the coffee table, everything. Everything was ugly.

I looked around me and I didn't recognize anything. Who could actually live happily here? I wondered. Playmobil figures? Show-home salesmen? No chaos, no mess, no whimsicality, no comfort. Nothing. Just decoration. Even worse: décor. I went into the kitchen, and there was nothing of me there either. It didn't remind me of anything. It didn't tell me any stories. I insisted, though. I bent down, opened doors, cupboards, drawers, but no, truly, there was nothing. No one.

The bedroom, maybe? I lifted the duvet, grabbed one pillow and then the other, buried my face in them, examined the sheets. Zilch. Nothing to indicate that human beings had ever lain there. Not the slightest smell of perfume, let alone sweat or saliva or cum. The bathroom? Toothbrushes, the oversized T-shirt Melanie slept in, our bath towels: silent. Who were these zombies, and what kind of existence was this, that we were leading, ultimately?

I didn't know what to grasp on to anymore. After the emotional overflow I'd more or less managed to unburden myself of upstairs, I was incapable of letting myself go again, and deep within me, in my nostrils and my throat, something kept me from making a sound. I clenched my fists and gritted my teeth and braced myself. I was ridiculous. A child. A stupid kid, temperamental and upset, but much too proud to show it.

Okay, well, now what? What could I smash to get myself noticed, huh?

I was frozen in that state of anxiety and violence and pow-erlessness when the doorbell rang.

Jesus, what the hell time was it? What the fuck was going on *now*?

Eight, Courtesy

A re you okay?"
Isaac looked like he didn't recognize me.

"Yann, are you okay? Is everything all right?"

I don't remember what I said to him. That I was tired, I think.

And it was true. I was tired.

Very tired.

Too tired.

It was myself I should have smashed. Too bad we only lived on the second floor.

"Here," he said, taking my hand. "I peeled it off for you. As a souvenir. You can order some, if you like, before . . . well . . . it's now or never . . . "

My Isaac. My prince. I gazed at him for a long time, to calm myself down. He looked exhausted.

Even the wings of his bow tie were drooping.

It's true, I did find him soothing, but in another sense he was way out of reality, too. Why had he brought me this now, really? As if it couldn't wait. And what wine was I going to order? I had no cellar, no money, no Alice, no almonds, no cast-iron casserole dish, no little daughters, no spices, no table-cloth, no wineglasses, nothing. For a guy who said he could sense everything and had an unfailing eye, this wasn't a very impressive performance.

To be fair, though, we'd drunk two and a half bottles of wine between the two of us. That can cause an error or two.

We stood on the landing since I couldn't reasonably invite him in, and it was at that precise second, just as I was thinking that, saying to myself on the subject of Isaac Moïse, who had become my friend, my treasured friend, *I can't reasonably invite him in*, that I finally grew up:

"Would it be all right if I came back upstairs with you, and borrowed Misia's little Fisher-Price tape recorder, the one that's in her bedroom in the middle of all the Barbies, if you don't mind?"

NINE, THE CROSSING

I had the murder weapon, but I needed the bullet. In this case, a cassette. That relic from the last century. That little black or clear plastic box containing a magnetic strip on which you could record sounds. That other world.

I wasn't going to ruin Misia's nursery rhymes, though.

I must still have one or two of them lying around somewhere, but where?

Diversion:

When I met Melanie I was sharing an apartment with two other shady characters near Barbès. The shared rooms were usually unbelievably messy, but I'd made a pretty cozy little bedroom for myself, I remember.

Lots of books, lots of music, ashtrays, eviscerated boxes sent from the country by my mom every week (Andouille sausage, *kouign-amann*, and *galettes au beurre*. Yeah, yeah, it's a lot, but that's just how my mom is. She's from Brittany.), a bunch of idiotic T-shirts, dirty underwear, mateless socks, burps, farts, wanking, dirty jokes, and even—miraculously, and far fewer, but a couple, anyway—girls who ended up there sometimes, plus everything that kept me treading water, stuck up on the walls: messages, pictures, faces, people's faces that I thought were beautiful or that I admired, architectural plans, prototypes, mock-ups, ideas, school essays, work reports, movie tickets, concert tickets, things I'd copied out of books, phrases instructing me to live with my head held high, facsimiles of drawings by Leonardo da Vinci, Arne Jacobsen, Le Corbusier, and Frank Lloyd Wright . . . and all those generous things adults write when you're still blowing bubbles in your milk with a straw, and when you go to Paris to study, and when you want to believe that you have some talent; but I won't let go of them, I'll never let go of them . . . and photos of my family, and my boats and my friends, and my dogs, living and dead . . . and posters of films and exhibitions and graphic artists and musicians and charismatic leaders . . . well, a bit of everything, really.

When we decided to live together to save on rent (my God, that sounds so sleazy—to have the pleasure of living together, let's say), we moved into a tiny one-bedroom apartment near the Gare de l'Est, and that was when I had to downsize.

I took a lot of it back to my parents' house and kept only the bare minimum necessary to finish my studies and keep myself clothed. But it was okay; we both worked and went out a lot; we loved each other, and besides, in the intervening years the Internet had become a giant wall on which I could pin, unpin, and admire anything that inspired me to my heart's desire.

Then when it became a question of us moving here to save on rent again (but let me be clear, we pay for the utilities, okay?!) (oh God, what have I become?), Melanie went through my clothes yet again, and because I was a grown man with a job now, there went my baggy T-shirts, my old sailor's jacket and my sweaters from the co-op, my Clarks, my trumpet, my cigarette papers, my sailor's caps, and my Tolkien books, because I wouldn't really be needing them anymore. Right, darling?

Fine, okay. She was right. We were living in a nice neighborhood now, and it really was great not to hear trains in the night anymore, or to be asked for a spare cigarette every two meters. If this was the price to pay, so be it. Quite apart from the fact that if I couldn't convince myself that I was an adult, who else would believe it? So, here we go, one more time, five fewer boxes. To be honest it never bothered me too much; I'd always liked to travel light, but the thing is . . . that now, well, I've got nothing left. Not even an audiocassette.

Well, too bad for Misia. I'll buy her a new one.

And then it comes back to me. When I sent my dear old Titine off to the junkyard last year, I saved everything in the glove compartment. Mandatory prehistoric radio, I must have a few tapes left, right?

I search.

And at the very back of the part of the closet that's been assigned to me, I find one. Just one. I don't recognize it and there's nothing written on it.

Okay. We'll see.

* * *

I take a shower and think. I put on boxer shorts, socks, and clean jeans, and I think. I look for an acceptable shirt and think. I tie my shoes and think. I make myself a coffee, thinking. A second coffee, thinking some more. A third, still thinking.

I think. I think. I think.

And when, from thinking so much, I don't have even a gram of alcohol left in my blood, when I don't have a single dry chest hair left and I'm as much on edge as a person can possibly be, I calm down.

I settle myself in the kitchen, light a candle like in Alice's kitchen because I noticed that candlelight makes people more attractive and more intelligent (mine is less elegant, of course, not a votive candle, just some of Melanie's "décor" bullshit that stinks of coconut) (but it'll do, it'll do) (not all in one night, Lady Life) (leave me a little something for what happens next, I beg you), turn out the light, sit down, and set the little tape recorder, covered with Strawberry Shortcake stickers, on the table in front of me.

I put my old cassette in and guess what I hear? Massive Attack.

God has a hell of a sense of humor. It would be hard to find anything more synchronistic. I could almost laugh about it, if I weren't so stressed. I rewind, grab the microphone, and I . . . I turn around, so I can't see my reflection in the mirror.

Because I'm disappointing even in my nice Sunday shirt, with my Home Shopping Network candlelight and my tiny microphone at the end of its yellow cord. No, trust me, it's better if I don't see that.

I clear my throat and press the big REC button (the blue one). The tape unspools, I clear my throat again, and I . . . I . . . uh . . . oh, shit. I rewind.

Okay, big guy, get on with it . . .

I take in a huge gulp of air, like the time I tried to swim across the whole jetty without coming up for air in front of all the girls at summer camp, and I press the blue button again.

I take the plunge:

"Melanie . . . Melanie, I can't stay with you. I . . . by the time you hear this message I'll be gone, because I . . . I don't want to live with you anymore."

(Silence.)

"I know I should have written you a letter, but I'm afraid I'd spell things wrong, and I know you, and I know that whenever you see a spelling mistake you immediately hate the person who made it, and I'd rather not take that risk.

"See, I'm recording this message so I can explain things to you, and I know this will be enough: Melanie, I'm leaving you because you hate people who misspell things.

"I'm sure that won't seem like much of a reason for you, but for me it's crystal clear. I'm leaving you because you don't cut people any slack, and because you never see what really counts in people. I mean, really, why does it matter if it's 'é' or 'er' or 'it's my sister's sweater' or 'its my sister's sweater,' you know? Why does it matter? Of course it catches a little in the ear and on the tongue . . . but, well, so what? It doesn't damage anything else, as far as I know. It doesn't damage people deep inside, their desires and their intentions. But yeah, actually, it ruins everything because you hate them even before they've had time to finish their sentence, and . . . uh . . . I . . . I'm getting off track. I didn't start out to talk to you about grammar.

"If I wanted to wrap this whole thing up super-fast I'd tell you that I'm leaving you because of Alice and Isaac. Because that would say it all. I'm leaving you because I met some people who made me understand how far off the mark we are as a couple. But I'm not going to talk to you about that. First because you'll be even ruder to them than usual, and second because I don't want to share them."

(Pause. The sound of a siren in the distance.)

"Among a million other things, they made me realize that . . . that we're playacting. We're lying. We're sweeping everything under the rug.

"I'm talking about love, Melanie. How long ago did we stop loving each other? Truly loving each other, I mean. Do you know? When did we start fucking instead of making love? It's always the same; I know how to give you pleasure and I give it to you; you know how to return the favor and you do it, but . . . what is that? What is it? We both come and then go to sleep? No, don't roll your eyes, you know I'm right. You know it.

"It's a sad place, our bed.

"Everything . . . everything has become sad.

"And it's not only that. Because I know you, and I know you've spent the last few minutes telling anyone who will listen that I'm a bastard, a real son of a bitch, and that really, when you think about everything you've done for me, and everything your family has done for me, the apartment, the rent, the vacations and all that, and my ears haven't stopped ringing, I'm going to give you my three reasons for leaving. Three little reasons, very clear, very straightforward. That way, at least the son of a bitch will be doing something more than just badmouthing you.

"I'm not telling you these reasons to justify myself; I'm telling them to you so you'll have something to chew over. Because you love chewing things over. Munching and chewing and harping ad nauseam, oh, people really suck, and you really don't deserve the stuff that happens to you, and . . . yeah, that's your thing, always blaming other people rather than questioning yourself. I don't hold it against you; I even envy you, you know. I'd love to be like that too, sometimes. It would make my life a lot simpler. I know it's because of your education, and the fact that you're an only child, and your parents have always idolized you and indulged all your little whims, and . . . well, all of that kind of spoiled you to the core, in the end.

"Even when it came to your stupid little Breton they turned a blind eye, which just goes to show! No, I know you're not actually cruel. But I'll give you the reasons anyway. It'll keep you busy. Both of you. You and your mother."

(Silence.)

"I'm leaving you because you always ruin the ends of movies for me at the theater. Every time. You do it to me every damn time.

"Even though you know it's important for me to sit in the dark for a few minutes longer, to get my emotions back under control, watching that string of unknown names on the screen, which are like a vital airlock for me between the dream and the street. I know you think it's boring, okay?, but I've told you a hundred times: go ahead without me, wait for me in the lobby, wait for me in a café, or just go to the movies with your friends, but don't do that to me anymore—don't ask me which restaurant we're going to after this, or talk to me about your coworkers or the fact that your shoes are pinching your feet, when the movie only just ended.

"Yeah, even a bad movie. I don't care. I'm going to stay until the very end. I'm not leaving until I'm sure they remembered to thank the mayor of Petzouille-les-Ouches and I've read the words 'Dolby' and 'Digital' at the end. Even a Danish film or a Korean one, and even if I don't understand a word, I need to do it. We've been going to the movies together for almost three years now, and for almost three years now I've felt you get irritated, physically irritated, from the very first line of the credits, and . . . and you . . . go fuck yourself, Melanie. Go to the movies with someone else. I didn't ask for much from you, and I even think that was the only thing I ever actually asked you to do, and . . . no."

(Silence.)

"The second thing is that you always eat my pieces of cake, and I can't take that anymore either. You claim to be watching your waistline, and you never order dessert, and every time mine arrives you grab my spoon and dig right in. It's just not okay. Even though you know the answer, you could ask my permission anyway, even if only to give me the illusion that I count a tiny bit. And plus you always eat the point, which is the best part of the cake. Especially with lemon tarts and cheesecakes and flan, which you know—or used to know, maybe—are my three favorite desserts.

"So there, now you can say to your friends: 'Can you believe it? After everything I've done for him, that asshole is leaving me over a piece of pie!,' because it'll be true. But make sure you specify that it's over the *point* of the piece of pie. The foodies will appreciate that.

"The last thing, and this is the most important one, I think, is that I'm leaving because I don't like the way you behave with my parents. God knows I haven't imposed them on you very much. How many times have they visited us since we've been together? Two? Maybe three? It doesn't matter; I'd rather not remember, because it would piss me off too much.

"I know they're less sophisticated than your parents. Less intelligent, less attractive, less interesting. I know their house is kind of small and there are a lot of doilies and bouquets of dried flowers, but you know, it's exactly the same thing as the spelling mistakes. It doesn't mean anything about them. Not anything important, anyway. The embroidery, the camper van in the back of the garden, the Venetian masks . . . all of that means they've got bad taste, sure, but it doesn't mean anything about who they are. About their tolerance and their kindness. Okay, my mother isn't as classy as yours. Okay, she doesn't know who Glenn Gould is. Okay, she always gets Manet and Monet mixed up and is afraid to drive in Paris, but when you deigned to come and see her, Mélanie, she went to the hairdresser just to honor you. I don't know if you noticed, but I did, and every time I think about that, every time, it . . . I don't know . . . it gets me right in the heart. That subservient way she acts with you, because you're thin and elegant, and because her son loves you, and . . . it may be bullshit, but that all gives you kind of a rarefied aura. She never goes to the hairdresser for my father, but for you, as a sign of respect, yes, she tries to make herself look pretty. And you can't possibly know how much that touches me. It probably doesn't mean much to you, though, right? You pick at your food, and turn up your nose every time your refined gaze happens to fall on their little shell knick-knacks or their set of *Encyclopedia Universalis* arranged in alphabetical order but never opened, but you know, when I was a kid, I never once saw my mother have fun, or go out shopping with her girlfriends, because my grandparents lived with us and she took care of them nonstop. And then when that was over, when she didn't have to cut their hair and fingernails anymore, or give them huge piles of potatoes or beans or whatever to peel, just so they'd feel like they were still useful; when she finally had some peace because they were in the goddamn cemetery at last, then boom, my sister's kids came to take their place. And you know what? I never heard her complain. Not once. I only ever saw her cheerful. Do you realize that?

"Always happy. Can you imagine the strength and the courage it takes in life for those two words to be combined within the same person for an entire lifetime? Fuck, but if that isn't the absolute height of class, I don't know what is. I'm going to confess something to you, Mélanie: I see no difference at all between my mother's cheerfulness and your Goldberg Variations played by your Gould. It's the same genius. And that woman, that queen, that queen among people, every time she calls me she asks about you, and . . . sometimes, I lie. Sometimes, before I hang up, I say 'Mélanie sends her love' or 'Mélanie sends hugs to you both,' and . . . well . . . I don't feel like lying anymore. So there you have it."

STOP (red button).

Whew.

I pull my head out from under the water and shake myself, like the handsome guys in Olympic swimming pools do.

I managed that pretty well, don't you think?

Where are those stuck-up girls from Camp Balou? Are they still there? Did they see me, at least?

Talk about an achievement . . .

I rewind just a little to make sure my demonic (nyuk nyuk) plan has worked. I do a test, and what do I hear? A voice like a constipated duck talking about a motor home . . .

Oh my God. I shut it off immediately.

It's distressing.

I'm distressed.

Jesus. It's hard to be yourself, when your self doesn't inspire you. It's so goddamned hard.

It's three-fifteen in the morning. I need another coffee.

I rinse my cup and raise my head, and I see it. My reflection. I see it.

I study it.

I think about Isaac, and Alice, and Gabrielle, and Schubert, and Sophia Loren, and Jacqueline's rear end, and her wall of solace.

I think about the Justes and I think about my parents.

I think about my job and my life and my meal vouchers and my comfort and my security. About the concept of commitment, my concept of commitment, cash, loot, dough, my benefits, my coworkers, my boss, their promises, and my work contract of indeterminate length.

Indeterminate. How did such a weak word take on so much value?

How?

I look at the toy sitting on my kitchen table, which has turned into a time bomb, and I hang my head again.

I don't like the idea of hurting Mélanie.

I don't love her enough anymore to keep up the pretense of being the nice little couple, but I love people too much to take the risk of hurting any of them, even the woman who takes away my movies, my desserts, and my childhood.

Yes. Even her.

It's damn hard to be cruel when you're nice. It's damn hard to leave someone. It's damn hard to come together the way you have to, to fall in line and speak with one voice when you don't like authority.

It's damn hard to give yourself enough importance to make a unilateral decision to change the life of another human being, and how pathetic is it to use the word "unilateral" at twenty-six years old in the kitchen of the small middle-class apartment of the old aunt of your absent girlfriend because you have a job to do at three o'clock in the morning?

Okay.

I feel sort of weak now.

What am I doing?

What am I doing with my life?

What am I doing with my Woof-Woofs?

Ah, fuck. What a pain in the ass.

And on top of everything else, it's making me use crude language.

Well, I'm fucking annoyed.

Let's sum up: What you have to do is be selfish. At least a little bit selfish. Otherwise you're not really alive, and in the end you'll die anyway.

Right.

Come on, my Yannou. Be brave. Get out your cock and your knife.

If you won't do it for yourself, do it for your cheesecakes.

Okay, but, stupid question: What do you do to be selfish when you just aren't? When you were raised in a world where other people counted more than you? And right on an ocean on top of that? You have to force yourself, right? I've tried really hard to get on board with the concept, as hard as I could: Me, Me, Me, Myself, My life, My happiness, My nest, but I just can't quite manage it. It doesn't interest me. It's like the Mickey Mouse watch: I waved my arm around to make my mom feel good, but I didn't really want it. I thought it was ugly.

Head down, jaw clenched, shoulders hunched, arms crossed, chest closed off, I ruminate.

I'm completely curled in on myself. Nothing is getting in from the outside, at all. I listen to the beating of my own heart, I breathe slowly, and I try not to let myself get screwed over by the fatigue and overindulgence that have evidently invited themselves to this particular pathetic summit.

I think.

I think about Isaac.

I don't see anyone but him, Isaac Moïse, who can take me from one side of the river to the other. I think about his face, his stories, his silences, his looks, his chuckling that is sometimes lecherous and sometimes virginal. His bad faith, his egotism, his generosity, the feeble excuse of the label a little while ago, and the way he'd had of taking my hand at just the moment when I really, really needed it.

I remember his words about politeness, and the tone of his voice when he said them. That gentleness. That gentleness and that cruelty. And I cling to that with all my strength.

I cling to it because it's the only absolute certainty I can still salvage from this mess, the only one. Yes. Yes, I am that. I am polite.

And because I'm polite, I end up unfolding my body and freeing myself finally from myself, and I press the green button one more time before stashing Misia's little tape recorder in the bottom of the fridge.

Hopefully Melanie won't feel the need to make fun of my pimply teenage music *and* my spinelessness. My *Paradise Circus* and my *Unfinished Sympathy*.

And while my old cassette records the sound of the cold, I get my stuff together.

* * *

My duffel bag is ready. Clean underwear, dirty underwear, shoes, razor, books, laptop, amps. That'll do.

One advantage of not liking yourself at all.

I get the tape recorder out of the fridge and, finally, push the EJECT button.

The compartment opens with a tortured little sound. *Tchak!* No more shackles.

I write her first name on the cassette and leave it on her pillow.

No. On the kitchen table.

If you can't be great, at least hang on to your decency.

* * *

I leave my key, slam the door behind me, and go up to the fourth floor.

I set my worldly possessions down at my feet, button my jacket, take out my gloves, sit down, and reunite with my wall.

I give myself up to it.

I wait for Alice or Isaac to open their door.

I need to give them back Misia's toy, and ask them one last question.

Eleven, the Horizon

My name is Yann André Marie Carcarec. I was born in Saint-Brieuc. I'll be twenty-seven in a few months. I'm five-foot-ten and I have brown hair and blue eyes. I have no criminal record and no distinguishing marks or scars.

I was an ordinary kid, a picture-perfect first communicant, the mascot of my Optimist Club, a quiet high school student, an honors graduate, a serious student, a sap who fell in love easily, and a faithful boyfriend.

I'd found a job without having discovered a passion for anything or a taste for a particular career. I'd just signed an indeterminate work contract that would have enabled me to get into a little bit of debt, so as to be able to get a little bit more in debt later on, and I was going out with a girl with a much more sophisticated background than mine. A girl who showed me the good things about the middle class, and its limits too. Who would have liked to smooth off my rough edges a bit, I know, but who unwittingly reinforced my natural tendency to be the big, boorish, untidy grandson of a fishing-boat captain. Who made me realize that my family was much less well-off than hers, but were much better people. That we paid less attention to style, but with us the chain was longer and the anchor was more secure. And that we didn't criticize other people nearly as much. That we were less obsessed with other people. Maybe because we were too stupid to see beyond the tips of our own noses, or maybe because at the tips of our noses there was the horizon.

Maybe that line, that infinite brushstroke that has separated sea from sky since the dawn of time, makes human beings less arrogant.

Maybe . . . I don't know . . . I'm definitely wrong to generalize, but . . . her father always got my first name wrong when he shook hands with me. Once it was Yvan, and once it was Yvon, and once it was Erwann. After a while it seemed pretty suspicious.

Now, his daughter, well, I loved her. I swear on my life, I loved her. But I didn't know what she wanted anymore. I disappointed her, and she disappointed me. We didn't dare admit it to each other, but our bodies were less polite than we were, and said things during the intimate times. Her smell, her taste, her breath, her sweat . . . they all ganged up against me. Everything changed so as to make me uncomfortable. And I'm pretty sure the same was true for her too. That soap and toothpaste and Eau Sauvage aftershave weren't covering up my discomfort anymore.

No, I'm not pretty sure. I know it.

I knew it.

Last night, I was alone. I was supposed to go to the movies, but there was a piece of furniture blocking my landing. It belonged to some neighbors that I hardly knew. People who lived two floors above me. A couple with two little girls. I offered to help them carry it up to their apartment, and I stayed with them until the early hours of the next morning.

The next morning—that is, this morning—I took a TGV and slept for the whole journey, and then a bus. An hour later I got off in a little square bordered with plane trees and went into a café. One that inspired me, and probably served consoling beverages to a lot of pétanque players in warm weather. After I finished my drink, I took a piece of paper out of my pocket and showed it around so that someone could tell me which direction to go, and the best road for hitchhiking.

It was looked at, and commented on, and agreed on, and it got pretty creased along the way.

You might have said it was a sort of map. A treasure map with a Southern Cross drawn in the middle. When I thanked them, they answered—or retorted, rather—"My pleasure." It made me jump.

I didn't wait very long. A young guy picked me up in his van. He was a mason. He built swimming pools, but it was the off-season now, so he was repairing vaults in the square. With his thumb and index finger extended, he sighted crows in the distance and brought them down with the word "Bang!" When he rolled himself a cigarette, he gripped the steering wheel between his knees and accelerated "to stabilize the vehicle." He was about to be a dad. Tonight, as a matter of fact. "Dang," he repeated, "dang, it was gettin' kinda nerve-wracking there . . . "

I smiled. Everything he said enchanted me. I loved his voice, his accent, his gift of gab. He was like the Al Pacino of the sticks. He must be about the same age as me, and he already had a van with his full name written on the side, and payroll taxes, and a family. It all seemed very exotic.

He dropped me off at a junction. He was sorry he couldn't take me all the way, but it was the bambino's fault. It was way over there, behind that hill. I could follow the road, but it would be quicker to cut across the fields. I thanked him. I was glad to have to walk. I had butterflies in my stomach. I told myself that the weight of my bag multiplied by the number of steps would eventually calm me down.

That was only one supposition among thousands of others blurring my vision.

I thought. I walked. I came up with a plan.

I imagined dialogues and replies and I walked faster and faster, trying to shake off my reservations.

My bag dug into my shoulder. There was a sort of little stone hut on the side of the road. The door opened easily. I left my books there.

I'd come back for them.
No one ever steals books.

I recognized the house. It was the same one as on my piece of paper. I left my bag outside, against one of the pillars by the gate. I entered a courtyard and headed for the tidiest of the group of buildings. The one with boots outside the front door and curtains at the windows. I knocked. No answer. A little louder. Still no one.
Damn. No more treasure.

I looked around me. I tried to understand where I was, how it all intertwined, and what the hell I was doing out here in the middle of nowhere. It was all a muddle.
Finally, the door opened behind me. I turned with a big smile, in lieu of a bouquet of flowers. (Unfortunately, that had wilted on my way here.)
Shit. I hadn't been expecting this at all.
Was she already at that point?
With her chin, she gestured toward an outbuilding. If I couldn't find that, all I had to do was go to the end of the path and look for a silhouette among the ridges.
"A silhouette, or a dog! If you grab the dog's tail, the gentleman won't be far behind."
She giggled.
I'd already gone three steps when she added:
"Remind him that Tom has practice at six o'clock. He'll understand! Thanks!"

I was disturbed. I always pay close attention to people, but I couldn't describe her to you, couldn't tell you anything about her face or her clothes or the color of her hair. The only thing about her I can remember is what I tried desperately not to look at: a pair of crutches.

Twelve, Terra Firma

What was I hoping for, exactly?
I don't know.
Something more meaningful.

A scene.
A beautiful scene.
Like something out of a movie, or a book.

A dazzling light, a sky in splendor, and a man standing there.
Yeah, that's it, a man standing with a . . . uh . . . some kind of shears in his hand.

And even an orchestra, while I'm at it. The trumpets from *Star Wars* or *The Ride of the Valkyries* or some crap like that.

Instead of that, I found myself in the doorway of a neon-lit shed, with a dog sniffing my crotch and the wankers from *Grosses Têtes* talking in the background.

Well played, Yannou. Well played.

That's not a camel, you idiot, it's a huge mutt!

I was squinting. I couldn't see anything.

"Is anyone there?"

On top of the hood of a tractor (I don't know if tractors have hoods and I'm not actually sure the machine in question was a tractor), a hairy silhouette straightened up, swearing.

"Goddamn," he grumbled, "you're the guy from the insurance company, right? Parker! Get down, dammit!"

Christ.

Can we do this over again without the dog?

He eyed me. You could tell that he was doubtful. I was a little unkempt for a Groupama agent.

When I didn't answer him, he turned away again.

"Can I help you?"

And then . . .

Then I let fly.

"No," I said to him. "No. You can't help me, but I can help
you. That's what I've come for. To help you. I'm sorry—hello. My
name is Yann. I . . . uh . . . (he had turned to me again) . . . last
night I met Isaac Moïse. He invited me to dinner and we drank
your wine, so he told me about you. He told me your history and
the . . . your wife's illness . . . and . . . and everything. He told me
that you didn't really believe in all this anymore, that you were
tired, and you'd decided to sell your business, and . . . (He was
staring at me now, and I was looking away so I wouldn't weaken.
Instead I counted the grease spots on the floor.) . . . and, no. You
won't sell. You won't sell because I quit my job for you. My job,
my life, my girlfriend, everything. No—I mean, not for you, for
me, and I . . . the . . . the Moïses are letting me stay in their house
until the summer, and I have two arms and two legs and my vac-
cinations are up to date, and I'm Breton and I'm hardheaded,
and I don't know anything about wine, but I'll learn. I learn fast
when I'm interested in something. Also I've got my license. I can
drive. I can run errands. I can cook the meals. I can drive Tom
to practice in a few minutes, if you want. I can do everything
your . . . that Ariane did, and that she can't do anymore for now.
And my parents will help you too. My dad's a CPA; he's retired
now but he can still crunch numbers just as fast, and he'll help
you as best he can, I know it. And he and my mother belong to a
kind of old people's club that travels Europe in motor homes,

and when it's time for the grape harvest they'll all come, you'll see. My parents, and their English and Italian and Dutch friends, and the whole gang. And I guarantee you that it'll be great, and those people won't charge you anything—they'll be proud to help, even! You can't sell, Pierre. What you've built so far is too beautiful for that. You can't throw the towel in now."

Silence.
A leaden silence.
An awful silence.
A sepulchral silence under the pale neon lights.

The man looked me straight in the eyes. His face didn't betray any emotion. Did he think I was crazy? Had he thrown in the towel a long time ago? Had he already signed something? Would he have preferred me to be from the insurance company? Or a liquidator? Or a notary clerk? Was he thinking up a reply scathing enough to send me back where I'd come from?

Was he racking his brain for words to remind me of the presumptuousness and arrogance it took for a gawky little Parisian middle-class liberal like me to come here like it was some adventure-quest?

Was he deaf? Or simpleminded, maybe? Uh . . . was he even the boss? Was he Pierre Cavanès? Did he even know my neighbors? Was he a farmhand? Or a tractor repairman, maybe?

Did he understand French?

Yoo-hoo, noble aborigine, you understand what me say to you?

It lasted for hours. *Dang, it was gettin' kinda dangerous there . . .* as my bricklayer friend would have said. I didn't know if I should take a step forward, or run away.

The problem was that I didn't want to leave. I'd traveled too far, and come such a long way, since last night. I couldn't.

*

The neon lights buzzed, the TV crackled, the dog counted grease spots, and I waited. I still had their label in my hand, and I was following my friend Isaac's instructions. I was giving destiny a nudge.

Was I ridiculous? Was the situation ridiculous? Too bad. Too bad for me. I might be asking to get kicked in the teeth again, but I wouldn't abandon my nest. Not again. Never again.

I'd had it up to here with being polite. It didn't pay.

"Just how much of that wine did you drink?" he asked me, finally.

His face was still impassive, but there, clinging to the question mark, was the faintest, tiniest teasing note.

I smiled.

He looked at me for a minute longer and then turned back to his engine.

"So Moïse sent you, then."
"The man himself."

Silence.
Long silence.
Grosses Têtes.
Awkwardness.

After . . . I don't know . . . ten, fifteen, twenty minutes, maybe, he looked up at me, and then, with a glance, indicated the steering wheel.

"Go ahead. Start it up, just to see."

And I started it up.
Just to see.

Born in Paris in 1970, Anna Gavalda's first published work was the critically acclaimed collection of short stories *I Wish Someone Were Waiting for Me Somewhere*, which sold over half a million copies in her native France and was published in the US by Riverhead in 2003. She is also the author of *Someone I Loved* and the international best-selling novel *Hunting and Gathering* (Riverhead, 2007), which was made into a film starring Audrey Tautou and Daniel Auteil. Gavalda lives in Paris.

EUROPA EDITIONS BACKLIST
(alphabetical by author)

Fiction

Carmine Abate
Between Two Seas • 978-1-933372-40-2 • Territories: World
The Homecoming Party • 978-1-933372-83-9 • Territories: World

Milena Agus
From the Land of the Moon • 978-1-60945-001-4 • Ebook • Territories: World (excl. ANZ)

Salwa Al Neimi
The Proof of the Honey • 978-1-933372-68-6 • Ebook • Territories: World (excl UK)

Simonetta Agnello Hornby
The Nun • 978-1-60945-062-5 • Territories: World

Daniel Arsand
Lovers • 978-1-60945-071-7 • Ebook • Territories: World

Jenn Ashworth
A Kind of Intimacy • 978-1-933372-86-0 • Territories: US & Can

Beryl Bainbridge
The Girl in the Polka Dot Dress • 978-1-60945-056-4 • Ebook • Territories: US

Muriel Barbery
The Elegance of the Hedgehog • 978-1-933372-60-0 • Ebook • Territories: World (excl. UK & EU)
Gourmet Rhapsody • 978-1-933372-95-2 • Ebook • Territories: World (excl. UK & EU)

Stefano Benni
Margherita Dolce Vita • 978-1-933372-20-4 • Territories: World
Timeskipper • 978-1-933372-44-0 • Territories: World

Romano Bilenchi
The Chill • 978-1-933372-90-7 • Territories: World

Kazimierz Brandys
Rondo • 978-1-60945-004-5 • Territories: World

Alina Bronsky
Broken Glass Park • 978-1-933372-96-9 • Ebook • Territories: World
The Hottest Dishes of the Tartar Cuisine • 978-1-60945-006-9 • Ebook •
Territories: World

Jesse Browner
Everything Happens Today • 978-1-60945-051-9 • Ebook • Territories:
World (excl. UK & EU)

Francisco Coloane
Tierra del Fuego • 978-1-933372-63-1 • Ebook • Territories: World

Rebecca Connell
The Art of Losing • 978-1-933372-78-5 • Territories: US

Laurence Cossé
A Novel Bookstore • 978-1-933372-82-2 • Ebook • Territories: World
An Accident in August • 978-1-60945-049-6 • Territories: World (excl. UK)

Diego De Silva
I Hadn't Understood • 978-1-60945-065-6 • Territories: World

Shashi Deshpande
The Dark Holds No Terrors • 978-1-933372-67-9 • Territories: US

Steve Erickson
Zeroville • 978-1-933372-39-6 • Territories: US & Can
These Dreams of You • 978-1-60945-063-2 • Territories: US & Can

Elena Ferrante
The Days of Abandonment • 978-1-933372-00-6 • Ebook • Territories: World
Troubling Love • 978-1-933372-16-7 • Territories: World
The Lost Daughter • 978-1-933372-42-6 • Territories: World

Linda Ferri
Cecilia • 978-1-933372-87-7 • Territories: World

Damon Galgut
In a Strange Room • 978-1-60945-011-3 • Ebook • Territories: USA

Santiago Gamboa
Necropolis • 978-1-60945-073-1 • Ebook • Territories: World

Jane Gardam
Old Filth • 978-1-933372-13-6 • Ebook • Territories: US
The Queen of the Tambourine • 978-1-933372-36-5 • Ebook • Territories: US
The People on Privilege Hill • 978-1-933372-56-3 • Ebook • Territories: US
The Man in the Wooden Hat • 978-1-933372-89-1 • Ebook • Territories: US
God on the Rocks • 978-1-933372-76-1 • Ebook • Territories: US
Crusoe's Daughter • 978-1-60945-069-4 • Ebook • Territories: US

Anna Gavalda
French Leave • 978-1-60945-005-2 • Ebook • Territories: US & Can

Seth Greenland
The Angry Buddhist • 978-1-60945-068-7 • Ebook • Territories: World

Katharina Hacker
The Have-Nots • 978-1-933372-41-9 • Territories: World (excl. India)

Patrick Hamilton
Hangover Square • 978-1-933372-06-8 • Territories: US & Can

James Hamilton-Paterson
Cooking with Fernet Branca • 978-1-933372-01-3 • Territories: US
Amazing Disgrace • 978-1-933372-19-8 • Territories: US
Rancid Pansies • 978-1-933372-62-4 • Territories: USA

Alfred Hayes
The Girl on the Via Flaminia • 978-1-933372-24-2 • Ebook •
Territories: World

Jean-Claude Izzo
The Lost Sailors • 978-1-933372-35-8 • Territories: World
A Sun for the Dying • 978-1-933372-59-4 • Territories: World

Gail Jones
Sorry • 978-1-933372-55-6 • Territories: US & Can

Ioanna Karystiani
The Jasmine Isle • 978-1-933372-10-5 • Territories: World
Swell • 978-1-933372-98-3 • Territories: World

Peter Kocan
Fresh Fields • 978-1-933372-29-7 • Territories: US, EU & Can
The Treatment and the Cure • 978-1-933372-45-7 • Territories: US, EU & Can

Helmut Krausser
Eros • 978-1-933372-58-7 • Territories: World

Amara Lakhous
Clash of Civilizations Over an Elevator in Piazza Vittorio •
978-1-933372-61-7 • Ebook • Territories: World
Divorce Islamic Style • 978-1-60945-066-3 • Ebook • Territories: World

Lia Levi
The Jewish Husband • 978-1-933372-93-8 • Territories: World

Valerio Massimo Manfredi
The Ides of March • 978-1-933372-99-0 • Territories: US

Leïla Marouane
The Sexual Life of an Islamist in Paris • 978-1-933372-85-3 •
Territories: World

Lorenzo Mediano
The Frost on His Shoulders • 978-1-60945-072-4 • Ebook •
Territories: World

Sélim Nassib
I Loved You for Your Voice • 978-1-933372-07-5 • Territories: World
The Palestinian Lover • 978-1-933372-23-5 • Territories: World

Amélie Nothomb
Tokyo Fiancée • 978-1-933372-64-8 • Territories: US & Can
Hygiene and the Assassin • 978-1-933372-77-8 • Ebook • Territories: US & Can

Valeria Parrella
For Grace Received • 978-1-933372-94-5 • Territories: World

Alessandro Piperno
The Worst Intentions • 978-1-933372-33-4 • Territories: World
Persecution • 978-1-60945-074-8 • Ebook • Territories: World

Lorcan Roche
The Companion • 978-1-933372-84-6 • Territories: World

Boualem Sansal
The German Mujahid • 978-1-933372-92-1 • Ebook • Territories: US & Can

Eric-Emmanuel Schmitt
The Most Beautiful Book in the World • 978-1-933372-74-7 • Ebook •
Territories: World
The Woman with the Bouquet • 978-1-933372-81-5 • Ebook • Territories:
US & Can

Angelika Schrobsdorff
You Are Not Like Other Mothers • 978-1-60945-075-5 • Ebook •
Territories: World

Audrey Schulman
Three Weeks in December • 978-1-60945-064-9 • Ebook • Territories: US
& Can

James Scudamore
Heliopolis • 978-1-933372-73-0 • Ebook • Territories: US

Luis Sepúlveda
The Shadow of What We Were • 978-1-60945-002-1 • Ebook • Territories:
World

Paolo Sorrentino
Everybody's Right • 978-1-60945-052-6 • Ebook • Territories: US & Can

Domenico Starnone
First Execution • 978-1-933372-66-2 • Territories: World

Henry Sutton
Get Me out of Here • 978-1-60945-007-6 • Ebook • Territories: US & Can

Chad Taylor
Departure Lounge • 978-1-933372-09-9 • Territories: US, EU & Can

Roma Tearne
Mosquito • 978-1-933372-57-0 • Territories: US & Can
Bone China • 978-1-933372-75-4 • Territories: US

André Carl van der Merwe
Moffie • 978-1-60945-050-2 • Ebook • Territories: World
(excl. S. Africa)

Fay Weldon
Chalcot Crescent • 978-1-933372-79-2 • Territories: US

Anne Wiazemsky
My Berlin Child • 978-1-60945-003-8 • Territories: US & Can

Jonathan Yardley
Second Reading • 978-1-60945-008-3 • Ebook • Territories: US & Can

Edwin M. Yoder Jr.
Lions at Lamb House • 978-1-933372-34-1 • Territories: World

Michele Zackheim
Broken Colors • 978-1-933372-37-2 • Territories: World

Alice Zeniter
Take This Man • 978-1-60945-053-3 • Territories: World

Tonga Books

Ian Holding
Of Beasts and Beings • 978-1-60945-054-0 • Ebook • Territories: US & Can

Sara Levine
Treasure Island!!! • 978-0-14043-768-3 • Ebook • Territories: World

Alexander Maksik
You Deserve Nothing • 978-1-60945-048-9 • Ebook • Territories: US, Can & EU (excl. UK)

Thad Ziolkowski
Wichita • 978-1-60945-070-0 • Ebook • Territories: World

Crime/Noir

Massimo Carlotto
The Goodbye Kiss • 978-1-933372-05-1 • Ebook • Territories: World
Death's Dark Abyss • 978-1-933372-18-1 • Ebook • Territories: World
The Fugitive • 978-1-933372-25-9 • Ebook • Territories: World
Bandit Love • 978-1-933372-80-8 • Ebook • Territories: World
Poisonville • 978-1-933372-91-4 • Ebook • Territories: World

Giancarlo De Cataldo
The Father and the Foreigner • 978-1-933372-72-3 • Territories: World

Caryl Férey
Zulu • 978-1-933372-88-4 • Ebook • Territories: World (excl. UK & EU)
Utu • 978-1-60945-055-7 • Ebook • Territories: World (excl. UK & EU)

Alicia Giménez-Bartlett
Dog Day • 978-1-933372-14-3 • Territories: US & Can
Prime Time Suspect • 978-1-933372-31-0 • Territories: US & Can
Death Rites • 978-1-933372-54-9 • Territories: US & Can

Jean-Claude Izzo
Total Chaos • 978-1-933372-04-4 • Territories: US & Can
Chourmo • 978-1-933372-17-4 • Territories: US & Can
Solea • 978-1-933372-30-3 • Territories: US & Can

Matthew F. Jones
Boot Tracks • 978-1-933372-11-2 • Territories: US & Can

Gene Kerrigan
The Midnight Choir • 978-1-933372-26-6 • Territories: US & Can
Little Criminals • 978-1-933372-43-3 • Territories: US & Can

Carlo Lucarelli
Carte Blanche • 978-1-933372-15-0 • Territories: World
The Damned Season • 978-1-933372-27-3 • Territories: World
Via delle Oche • 978-1-933372-53-2 • Territories: World

Edna Mazya
Love Burns • 978-1-933372-08-2 • Territories: World (excl. ANZ)

Yishai Sarid
Limassol • 978-1-60945-000-7 • Ebook • Territories: World (excl. UK,
AUS & India)

Joel Stone
The Jerusalem File • 978-1-933372-65-5 • Ebook • Territories: World

Benjamin Tammuz
Minotaur • 978-1-933372-02-0 • Ebook • Territories: World

Non-fiction

Alberto Angela
A Day in the Life of Ancient Rome • 978-1-933372-71-6 • Territories:
World • History

Helmut Dubiel
Deep In the Brain: Living with Parkinson's Disease • 978-1-933372-70-9 •
Ebook • Territories: World • Medicine/Memoir

James Hamilton-Paterson
Seven-Tenths: The Sea and Its Thresholds • 978-1-933372-69-3 • Territories:
USA • Nature/Essays

Daniele Mastrogiacomo
Days of Fear • 978-1-933372-97-6 • Ebook • Territories: World • Current
affairs/Memoir/Afghanistan/Journalism

Valery Panyushkin
Twelve Who Don't Agree • 978-1-60945-010-6 • Ebook • Territories:
World • Current affairs/Memoir/Russia/Journalism

Christa Wolf
One Day a Year: 1960-2000 • 978-1-933372-22-8 • Territories: World •
Memoir/History/20th Century

Children's Illustrated Fiction

Altan
Here Comes Timpa • 978-1-933372-28-0 • Territories: World (excl. Italy)
Timpa Goes to the Sea • 978-1-933372-32-7 • Territories: World (excl. Italy)
Fairy Tale Timpa • 978-1-933372-38-9 • Territories: World (excl. Italy)

Wolf Erlbruch
The Big Question • 978-1-933372-03-7 • Territories: US & Can
The Miracle of the Bears • 978-1-933372-21-1 • Territories: US & Can
(with **Gioconda Belli**) *The Butterfly Workshop* • 978-1-933372-12-9 •
Territories: US & Can